One Man Left

A Joel Franklin Mystery, Volume 12

Ron Finch

Published by Ron Finch, 2024.

This is a work of fiction. Similarities to real people, places, or events are entirely coincidental.

ONE MAN LEFT

First edition. March 13, 2024.

Copyright © 2024 Ron Finch.

Written by Ron Finch.

Books by Ron Finch

The Joel Franklin Mystery Series:

    Lightning at 200 Durham Street
    Where's the Rest of the Body?
    Terror on the Way
    One Foot Out of the Grave
    It's Your Own Fault
    I Told You! I'm Innocent!
    24 Booke Street
    Who's Crazy?!
    Who Stole My Car?
    Firebug
    Sins of the Past
    One Man Left

Dr. Shitz:

    Dr. Shitz and the Wayward Ghost

Important Quotes

"There are more things in heaven and earth, Horatio, than are dreamt of in your philosophy." – William Shakespeare

"Listen!" – Everyone's mother

"Believe nothing you hear, and only one half that you see." – Edgar Allen Poe

"Don't believe everything you think." – Allan Lokos

"Do what you can. Don't do what you can't." – Something I say several times a week, sometimes to myself.

Main Characters

The Franklins
  Joel Franklin (b. 1911) – Detective, London Police
  Georgie Franklin (née Harkness) (b. 1913) – Joel's wife
  Annie (b. 1936) – their daughter
  Arthur Edward (b. 1939) – their son

London Police Force
  Chief Lawrence Bedgegood – chief of the LPF
  Inspector Gerald O'Neill – Joel's immediate supervisor
  Inspector Thomas Simpson – head of the LPF Special Services squad
  Constable Brian Carmichael – Joel's assistant
  Constables Doug Johnson and Freddy Brown – two of Simpson's men
  Constables Henderson and Bartlett – being trained in forensic science

Dr. Plimpton's Séance Group
  Dr. Harold Plimpton
  Simon and Simone – Dr. Plimpton's assistants
  Celeste Bedgegood
  Martha Brightman
  Irma Chavin
  Marian McKelvie
  Alice Mulder

Barbara Watkins

The Group of Six
Compton Bedgegood (deceased)
Arthur Brightman
Edward Chavin
Ambrose 'Butch' McKelvie
Jordan Mulder
Roger Watkins

Celeste Bedgegood's Household Staff
Sarah Olson – the housekeeper
Violet Murphy – the cook
Horace Walker – the gardener
Paul – Celeste's informal chauffeur

Barbara Watkins's Household Staff
Jason – the butler
Rodney – butler's aide

The Donnellys
Kurtis Donnelly – Celeste Bedgegood's nephew
Sally Donnelly – Kurtis's wife
Kitty – the elder daughter
Stella – the younger daughter

Other Notables
   Dick Robinson – coroner for the city of London
   Dr. Alfred Khryscoff – prominent psychiatrist, Joel's friend and mentor
   Gwen Cummings – Dr. Khryscoff's fiancée

Essences
   Dora

Thursday, June 8th, 1939

These are lovely old homes, I thought as I stood in front of Celeste Bedgegood's house on Central Ave., a three-storey red brick Victorian building.

Since moving to London, Ontario, in September of last year, I'd discovered that the city had several fine residential neighbourhoods. The garage of Celeste Bedgegood's home alone was almost as big as the house my wife, Georgie, and I were renting on Princess Ave. in London East.

I walked up the four steps onto the front porch, which extended the width of the house. White wooden columns, spaced about ten feet apart, extended from the floor of the veranda to the roof above, a height of about twelve feet. A porch swing hung to one side; potted plants provided some colour.

I walked across the porch to the front door, a large, solid-looking barrier—most likely made of oak—with a unique design carved into it. In the centre of the door, about four feet up, was a large brass door knocker.

I reached for the knocker and hesitated, somewhat intimidated. The knocker was a mould of a stern, matronly woman's face. There was a sort of wreath attached by a hinge where her ears should have been. I recalled seeing this ancient visage in one of Dr. Khryscoff's books about Roman mythology. Sulis Minerva, she was called. Unfortunately, I couldn't remember what she was goddess of.

I checked the time on my pocket watch. It was ten o'clock. The chief had told me not to be late. I grasped the knocker and banged it loudly three times.

As I waited, I looked around, enjoying the warm, sunny weather and taking in the beautiful landscaping of the surrounding properties. Compared to some of the places I'd been in my role as a detective, Celeste's neighbourhood was an earthly paradise.

An old woman, about four foot ten and weighing perhaps ninety-five pounds—about as much as the door—answered. She gave me a look that would intimidate most people; it certainly intimidated me.

"Who are you?" she asked in a demanding voice.

"My name is—" That was as far as I got before the door crashed shut in my face.

I stood there, dumbfounded. Had Chief Bedgegood forgotten to tell his aunt I was coming?

I was still standing there, debating what to do, when the door suddenly swung open.

It was the old woman again, looking just as intimidating, but now holding an ear trumpet. "Sorry," she said, "I forgot my hearing aid. Who are you, and what do you want?"

"My name is—"

And again, that was as far as I got before she said, "Detective Joel Franklin."

I must have looked as bewildered as I felt because she gave me a curious look and said, "Do you forget your name often?"

I knew there was little to be gained by attempting to explain to her that she hadn't given me time to say it, so, instead, I smiled at her and said, "Not usually."

"Come in," she said, "it's already one minute after ten o'clock."

I followed her through a large foyer dominated by a gilt-framed mirror, past a ticking grandfather clock which now said 10:02, below a grand staircase leading up to the second floor, and into a large sitting room off to the left of the main entrance. A quick calculation told me the rooms had fourteen-foot ceilings.

The sitting room had a marble fireplace, a bay window overlooking the street, antique furniture, and an expensive-looking rug. A large, framed oil painting hung over the fireplace, the portrait of a frowning, older Victorian gentleman with a monocle and a bushy moustache. The resemblance to Chief Bedgegood, the head of the London Police Force, was striking.

Celeste crossed the room and sat on a small but beautiful chesterfield. Arranging her skirts, she said, "Please have a chair."

I approached the nearest chair, a comfortable-looking armchair, and seated myself. She said, "Not that chair," and waved me out of it. "Are you sure you're a detective? Did you not notice which ear I'm using my ear trumpet with?"

Embarrassed, I got up and took a chair on the other side of her, a much less comfortable one. I didn't tell her she hadn't indicated which ear she was going to use until I sat down. I had a grandmother of my own in Chaseford, and I knew better. As long as I didn't disagree with her, and humoured her a little, I was certain we would get along.

"Chief Bedgegood asked me to come and see you about a possible crime," I said.

The old woman stared at me.

"Would you, ah, please tell me a bit about it?" I continued.

"Speak up, young man," she said. "Don't mumble. I can't hear you."

She made a face, inspected her ear trumpet, and muttered, "Oh, never mind. I forgot I put a piece of cotton batting in that ear."

She switched the ear trumpet to her other ear.

"Excuse me," I said and got up and went to the chair on the other side of her, the comfortable armchair, and asked her again about the crime.

"Bubbles worries about me too much," Celeste said, "but he's a good nephew, and he's been very helpful since my husband died."

"Excuse me?" I said, quite certain I'd misheard her. *Bubbles?*

"I said he's been very helpful since my husband died," Celeste repeated more loudly. "Are you sure you don't need an ear trumpet?"

That wasn't the part I'd wanted her to repeat, but I didn't have to wait long for clarification.

"When you see Bubbles, tell him not to worry so much," she said loudly, as if I were the one hard of hearing.

There was no doubting it this time. I looked down at my notepad, holding the pencil to my lip. "Bubbles" was too wildly inappropriate a name for my commander-in-chief. It was all I could do not to laugh. I wanted nothing so much as to be able to tell Det. O'Neill, or anyone else, this remarkable nickname, but I knew I couldn't, not until after my retirement thirty-five years from now.

Celeste looked at me sharply and said, "Do you have to sneeze young man? Why are you making that face? Don't get anything on my furniture."

"No, ma'am, I'm fine," I said, composing myself. "I just, ah, had a thought."

"Well, try not to have too many of them," said Celeste. "They look painful."

We were both silent for a moment. She looked around the room, as if hoping to find someone more interesting to talk to.

"I guess I should tell somebody about the theft," she said finally, "and since you're a detective, I might as well tell you."

Involuntarily, I looked at the clock on the mantlepiece. It was already seven after ten. I was glad we were finally getting under way.

"My house was broken into, Detective, and a beautiful British biscuit box was stolen. Now, mind you, I never told Bubbles that somebody broke into the house, so don't you go upsetting him," warned Celeste. "Find a good way to break the news to him. He worries too much about me already."

I made a note in my book. Now I knew I was involved in The Case of the Stolen British Biscuit Box. Not my most important case to date, but certainly a nice change from kidnapping, arson, and murder.

"Could you give me a description of the biscuit box?" I said.

"It's not just a 'biscuit box,' young man," said Celeste severely and eyeing me with disapproval. "It's a rare, antique British biscuit box."

"I'm sorry, I haven't seen many British biscuit boxes. I didn't realize how valuable it was," I said.

"It's valuable," she said nodding, "but not near as valuable as the deeds and other documents it contains."

Ah. The case had suddenly become more interesting.

"Would you please show me where the box was stolen from?" I asked.

She handed me the ear trumpet, got up slowly and with some effort, and said, "Follow me."

Still holding the trumpet, I followed her from the sitting room. Her home had a centre floor plan with one minor difference: the main hallway was offset to one side of the centre of the house, which meant that the rooms on the right side of the hallway were only about ten feet wide, while the rooms to the left of the hall, where we had been sitting, were about twenty-five feet in width.

Aunt Celeste led me down the main hall past two rooms, one to the left and one to the right, and we entered the next room to the right. It wasn't a very large room, but it was very nicely furnished as an office. Directly across from where we stood in the doorway was a window that looked out onto a wide side yard in the centre of which was a sundial. There were bookshelves to our left, along the wall closest to the back of the house. An ornate desk was placed in such a way that, when you sat in the chair at the desk, the bookshelves were behind you. On the wall opposite the desk, beside a large, landscape painting, was a door to a closet. Celeste opened the closet and showed me the shelves that were built on the walls on each side. The shelves were filled with carved and inlaid wooden boxes and decorated metal tins. On the third shelf from the bottom there was an empty space. She pointed at the space and said, "That's where I kept my special box."

I hastily returned her ear trumpet.

"Is it the only box that went missing?" I asked.

"Yes," said Celeste, shutting the door.

"Do you keep the door to your office locked, or the door to the closet locked?" I asked.

"No, there's never anyone in the house but me and sometimes Bubbles. I don't lock the doors inside my house; if I did, I'd never be able to get in the rooms because I'd never find the keys," she said with a look that suggested I had better think twice about giving her advice.

I thought again about the size of the rooms and the number of rooms there must be. It was hard to believe she lived in this big house all by herself.

"So, for someone to get into this room, they would either have to be in the house visiting you, or they would have to come through that window," I said, pointing.

"You're right, young man," she said with the first trace of visible agitation. "It's very upsetting. The morning after the last séance was held here, a couple of weeks ago, my housekeeper, Sarah Olson, reported to me that my office window was open. She said it must have been open all night because it had rained during the night, and the windowsill and the carpet below the window were damp."

Ah, the housekeeper. Things were slowly falling into place. I looked at the window and sill but saw no sign of tampering from inside.

"So, you have people that help you with the house, do you?" I said.

"Of course," she said indignantly. "You don't think I can look after a big house like this by myself, do you? I'm not as young as I used to be."

"Would I be able to get a list of these people?" I said, taking out my notebook. "May I use the desk?"

"Certainly," said Celeste, nodding magnanimously. "Let me see," she said when I'd settled myself. "Violet Murphy does the cooking. She arrives about eleven in the morning and stays until seven in the evening. Horace Walker looks after the gardening, the grass, and the snow. In the winter he comes when he's needed, but this time a year he comes every Monday and Thursday from two in the afternoon until five o'clock, suppertime. Sarah Olson, the one I just told you about, does the house cleaning and laundry. She's here every day from one o'clock until eight o'clock most evenings."

I jotted everything down. Now I had something to work with.

"I may not interview them all today, if that's okay," I said, "but I will have them all interviewed by Monday at the latest."

"That's not a problem," said Celeste. "Just remember not to get Bubbles all upset. He doesn't know all those important papers are missing."

Again, I had to suppress a smile.

"I want you to think back over the last month or two," I said. "Have you had any company at all other than—" I paused for a moment; I didn't want to say the B word "—your nephew?"

"I told you before," said Celeste with a snap in her voice, "no one has been here, aside from our little séance group. Don't keep asking me the same questions. It makes me impatient."

"Do you conduct these ... séances?" I asked incredulously.

"Don't be a fool," Celeste said. "Of course not. Dr. Harold Plimpton does. He's famous around the world, you know."

I added another name to my list.

"How do I get in touch with this Dr. Plimpton?"

"I'll give you a copy of his letter of introduction. It's a special letter, but he gave me two of them," Celeste said proudly.

She went to the office closet, opened the door, and reached down to the second lowest shelf and picked up a unique looking container. She set the container on the desk, opened the lid, and took out a letter.

She handed me the letter and said, "That should help you locate Dr. Plimpton."

I thanked her, but I couldn't help remarking on the unusual container. "That's an interesting box," I said.

"Yes," Celeste said, "it's a 1905 British biscuit box. That one originally contained peppermint lumps."

I decided to leave. A retreat at this point in the investigation would be honourable. I had collected far more information than I had originally anticipated about a matter that was far more serious than Bubbles—er, Chief Bedgegood—had led me to believe.

"You'll never guess who I saw today," I said to my wife, Georgie, at lunch as I sat down at the kitchen table and began making myself a sandwich.

"It was almost Franklin child number two," Georgie said with a grunt as she eased herself heavily into the chair and patted her enormous belly. "Gave me quite a scare."

I almost dropped my sandwich but managed to keep just about everything on my bread.

"False alarm," said Georgie, smiling winsomely.

Georgie was in the last weeks of her pregnancy, so, whenever possible, I've been going home at lunchtime. Of course, I'm still away for most of the day, which has me on tenterhooks. Georgie seems to be handling the stress better than I am, but, unlike me, she has a plan. In the event that something should happen while I'm at work, our next-door neighbour, Kay Dunnigan—whom we refer affectionately to as Auntie Kay—told us she would get a taxi and take Georgie and Annie, our not-quite-three-year-old daughter, to the hospital. It's less than ten days until Gwen and Alfred's wedding, and Georgie is bound and bent she will be there as the matron of honour.

"Tell me, who did you see?" said Georgie, filling her plate with pickles.

"Chief Bedgegood's aunt."

"Really?" she said, intrigued.

I related a bit about my meeting with Aunt Celeste. When I mentioned her collection of British biscuit boxes, Georgie's eyes widened, and she said, "Oh, they're so adorable!"

Fortunately, I hadn't yet expressed my opinion about them. Nor had I made the terrible mistake of calling them cookie tins. So far today, I was doing better than I normally do at thinking before I speak. Usually, I speak first and apologize later.

Annie, who had been stacking cucumber slices with a good deal of concentrated attention, chimed in and said, "Oh, Mommy, Daddy is talking about pretty biscuit boxes, like the ones Auntie Kay has on top of her china cabinet!"

Georgie gave me a smug look. Even Annie knew more about British biscuit boxes than I did.

I had more than British biscuit boxes to relate, but I concentrated on chewing each bite of my sandwich. If my mouth was full, I couldn't talk.

Soon, lunch was over, and I was on my way back out the door. It had been a real struggle, but I'd managed to keep Chief Bedgegood's secret pet name to myself. The last thing I needed was my daughter calling my boss Bubbles at the next police picnic.

After lunch, I drove directly over to Celeste Bedgegood's home on Central Ave. I rapped on the door with the knocker, and this time the door was answered by a tall, robust woman with red hair who welcomed me inside. She was wearing a conservative grey dress and appeared to be in her mid forties.

She introduced herself as Violet Murphy, and added with a polite bow, "Ma'am said you'd be back, sir. She couldn't remember your name, but said you were a very young detective who didn't know which side to sit on. It makes no sense to me, but I'm guessing it does to you."

"The name is Joel Franklin." I declined to explain Celeste's comment, which would have taken too long to explain, and instead asked, "Is there a convenient place I could interview you, Violet?"

"Ma'am said you'd be using her office for interviews," said Violet. "I'm not sure what it's about. Was a crime committed here?"

"I'll explain what I can," I said, following her down the hall to the office.

I shut the door behind us.

"To answer your question, Violet, yes, there was a theft from the house." I decided I wouldn't give specifics to anyone. It's the best way to run an investigation if you can do it. By not mentioning what had been stolen, I might even find out that something else had been stolen.

"I didn't steal nothing, sir," said Violet.

"No one's accusing you of anything," I said. "It's standard procedure to interview everyone who works at a place where something has been stolen. Please take a seat."

I sat down at the desk, and she took a chair nearby.

"I'll answer your questions as best I can, sir," she said. "Ma'am is very generous. She said she wouldn't deduct the time I spent talking to you from my time worked. But she did ask me to tell you not to take too long, if you could help it, sir."

I was hardly surprised by this communication.

"This won't take long if you cooperate, Violet," I said, taking out my notebook.

I started the interview by saying, "I need honest answers to my questions. It's difficult enough to solve a crime with all the right answers; when people give you misleading or false information, or leave information out, it becomes much more difficult, and I have to pry a lot deeper. That can be uncomfortable for everyone. I know you won't do that, Violet, but I tell you that because it's against the law not to answer to the best of your ability."

"Aye sir—I mean, yes sir. It's all a mystery to me," Violet said, her Irish accent slipping through. "Ask me your questions, I'll give you my answers."

I like to start every interview with a couple of easy questions that demonstrate the connection between the person I'm interviewing and the person or the crime I'm investigating. Then I drop in a difficult question as it allows me to quickly determine how forthcoming the person I'm interviewing will be.

"Are you a Canadian citizen, Violet?" I asked.

"I am, sir. My parents came from Ireland, but I was born in Canada."

"How long have you worked for Mrs. Bedgegood?"

"It's at least seven years now. I began working for her after her husband died."

"What is she like to work for?" I asked.

"There's worse to work for. She can be confusing at times. And she's very particular. If she doesn't like something, like something I've prepared for dinner, she'll tell me in no uncertain terms, and I have to prepare something else."

"How do you feel about that?"

Violet hesitated.

"Don't worry, I'm not going to tell her what you said. Just be honest," I said.

"Well, the first couple of times it happened, I was a wee bit angry. To be honest, I almost quit, sir. She has a tone, you know. Then I realized it was just her way, and after all I was supposed to be preparing stuff she wanted to eat and not food I wanted to prepare."

"If you had quit, what would she have said?"

"Goodbye. I don't mean that as a joke, sir, it's the way she is. I needed a job, though, so I didn't quit."

"Do you ever have to prepare food for parties or special events?"

"She doesn't hold many special events. Keeps to herself, mostly. If a lot of people are coming, she lets me hire two or three other people to help in the kitchen, and I supervise."

"What was the last time that happened? I mean an event where you had to hire people to help you."

"It was one of those meetings where you sit around a table and call spirits," said Violet, failing to entirely conceal her disapproval.

"A séance," I said. "What did you think of the séance?"

"It's a bunch of hokum, if you ask me," she said. "First, I don't believe in that kind of stuff. Once you're dead, you're dead. I say thank heavens for that. I sure wouldn't want my first husband hanging around talking to me."

"How many people were here at the séance?"

"Five women—older ladies, Mrs. Bedgegood's age—plus Celeste, sat at the table. Dr. Plimpton had two assistants with him. That's right, I remember now, we needed food for nine."

"What's your opinion of Dr. Plimpton?"

"I didn't much like him, if I'm going to be honest," said Violet. "I don't think he's a real doctor, and if you're not a real doctor, and you use that title, then I don't think you're very trustworthy. I think the only spirit he believes in is money."

"Where did the séance take place?"

"It was in the big drawing room, on the left side of the hall as you come in the front door."

"The kitchen is along the back of the house, isn't it?" I said. "So you can see all along the hallway up to the front door from the kitchen when you're working in there."

"That's right," Violet replied.

"The night of the séance, did you see anybody come up the hall and go into Celeste's office?"

"I wasn't watching the hallway all the time, sir, but I did see a couple of people go into the office," said Violet.

"Who went into the office that night?"

"Dr. Plimpton went in just before the séance, and one of his assistants went in right after the séance. Oh, I almost forgot, Mrs. Chavin went in the office just before the end of the séance."

"Aside from the séance, and not counting the people who work here, in the last six weeks have there been any repairman or any other visitors to the house?"

"No, just her nephew."

"You're referring to Chief Bedgegood?" I asked.

"No, sorry, sir. I forgot. The chief drops in at least once a week. I'm talking about her nephew Kurtis Donnelly. I was thinking anyone out of the ordinary."

"Thank you for your time, Violet. I appreciate your candour."

"Sorry, sir?"

I realized from her puzzled look she was wondering what a candour was. I tried to recover by saying, "I meant thank you for being very straightforward."

"Oh, of course, sir. Will there be anything else?"

"No, you can return to your duties," I said.

She wished me a good day and left.

I had obtained quite a bit of information from Violet, so I decided I would leave the other interviews for another day.

Friday, June 9th

Chief Bedgegood had asked me to visit his aunt Celeste on Wednesday, and now more than an entire day had passed. I knew that when I reached the police station this morning, he would want to see me right away. The chief can be a very demanding taskmaster. When he asks you to do something, he expects results immediately. It's really not good for his blood pressure, and it's really not good for your blood pressure.

As I entered the detective department at the station, Inspector O'Neill, my immediate supervisor and friend, stuck his head out of his office door. With a sympathetic smile, he said, "Chief Bedgegood wants to see you, pronto."

Reluctantly—but rapidly—I made my way to the chief's office. As I reached for the door handle, the chief barked, "Come in, Joel, I've been waiting for you."

I slipped through the door and shut it behind me. He was sitting hunched over his desk, writing something on a sheet of paper.

"Sit down and tell me what you learned from my aunt Celeste," he said without looking up.

"Well, sir," I said, sliding into a chair. "I learned that your aunt Celeste is very sharp for being eighty-nine years old."

"I know that," the chief said impatiently, glancing up from the paper. "Don't butter me up, Detective. What did she tell you?"

"You've put me in a quandary, sir."

"How's that?" he asked irritably.

"I'm not supposed to upset you," I said as deferentially as I could. "Your aunt told me I may tell you what happened, but I have to explain the events in a way that won't cause you any distress."

Chief Bedgegood puffed up his cheeks, ran his hands through his hair, let out a sigh, and settled deeper into his chair.

"I know what you're telling me, Joel. That woman can be very difficult. I know better than to cross her. So, you tell me what you have to, and I will get as angry as I want to here in my office, but I'll pretend to her that I'm not too upset."

It seemed I was to be spared the wrath of one Bedgegood at the cost of being exposed to the wrath of the other.

"Your aunt told me that someone has stolen something from the office in her home," I said.

I could see the pink turning to red in the chief's face.

"What was stolen?" he asked in a somewhat louder voice.

"The thief took her favourite British biscuit bo—"

That was as far as I got.

"*You're making a melodrama out of the theft of a cookie tin?!*" he bellowed.

At this point in our conversation, I thought it wise not to explain that 'cookie tin' was not an appropriate appellation for the missing item. I would leave that correction to his aunt Celeste. Or to my wife, Georgie, or to my daughter, Annie.

"*This is about stolen cookies?!*"

Despite the verbal barrage, I continued stoically.

"That's not all, sir. I believe the thief was after the contents of the biscuit box—not cookies, but your aunt's most valuable documents, including the deed to her property, her will, and other assorted papers."

"*What?!*" Chief Bedgegood shouted at a volume that caused the glass in the door to rattle.

His personal secretary appeared at the door in a flurry, out of breath and alarmed, to see if he was okay. He obviously wasn't, and when his secretary saw the poinsettia colour of his face, she made a sort of high-pitched squeak and quickly retreated. No doubt to go on an early lunch.

Fortunately, I've always enjoyed a good bollocking. The appearance of being grievously wounded afterwards doesn't hurt, either. Georgie tells me it makes me look like a puppy dog.

Chief Bedgegood must've noticed the puppy-dog look on my face because he shut his eyes and took three deep breaths. Soon, he'd recovered enough that his voice sounded normal except for a kind of strangling sound in the back of his throat. "I'm sorry, Joel," he said with becoming contrition. "I know none of this is your fault."

"This one hit close to home," I said tactfully. "Your aunt seems to be taking it well, and she was very cooperative. I now have a list of people to interview. I've already interviewed her cook, Violet Murphy, and I have some contact information for several of the others. I'll keep you up to date on the investigation, sir."

"Yes, that's good," said the chief. "Perhaps ... it would be wise if I don't have another update ... today."

I silently concurred. I also decided it would be wise not to mention, for the moment, that the theft had likely occurred during a séance that his aunt had hosted at her residence.

I quickly excused myself and started back to my desk in the detective section of the police department. As I walked past Insp. O'Neill's door, he grinned and said, "I'm glad to see you're still on your feet, Joel. Better yet, you're smiling."

"Of course I'm smiling," I said, smiling even wider. "I'm no longer in the chief's office."

"I couldn't use my telephone while he was busy shouting at you," said O'Neill, picking up the telephone handset. "I'd never be able to hear the person on the other end of the line."

He started dialing a number.

"You may not believe this," I said, "but the chief and I are still on good terms." Then, for fun, I added, "Don't worry, I did my best to defend you."

O'Neill paled a little but couldn't reply as the person on the other end of the line had already answered his call. I kept walking. And smiling.

Once at my desk, I telephoned the number for Dr. Harold Plimpton recorded in the letter that Celeste Bedgegood had given me. An affected female voice answered, "Plimpton residence, how may I help you?"

"Could I speak to Dr. Plimpton, please," I said.

"I'm sorry, but Dr. Plimpton is absent on an extended foreign consultation. If you would identify yourself and leave your phone number, I will have him contact you," she said.

"Perhaps I could come and see him," I said. "What's his address?"

I flipped open my notebook.

"You've called his estate in Grosse Pointe, Michigan," said the woman. "I am not at liberty to give you his address. Dr. Harold Plimpton is much in demand around the world, as he is an expert spiritual guide and one of the few Doctors of Thaumaturgy in the world. You must surely be aware that, for a consultation to be relevant, it must be held in an environment familiar to the spirit."

I was quickly getting out of my league here, and I realized that I would also need to consult a dictionary. I wasn't sure if I'd written down the big 'T' word right. My chances of seeing Dr. Harold Plimpton would vanish if I used my title as Det. Joel Franklin, so I said, "Please ask Dr. Plimpton to contact Joel Franklin. I'm an acquaintance of Celeste Bedgegood of London, Ontario." I gave her my home phone number.

As soon as I hung up, I hastily phoned Georgie at home and said, "I'm expecting a very important call today in connection with the case I'm working on. Please don't let Annie answer the phone, and when you do answer the telephone, would you please say, 'Joel Franklin residence, how may I help you?'"

There was a pause at the other end of the line, and then Georgie said, "What have you done, Joel?"

"Uh, well ... I may have implied I was a good personal friend of a wealthy and influential member of our community."

"Joel!"

"I didn't lie, dear. I said I was an acquaintance, which is true. We are acquainted."

I could practically see the expression on my wife's face.

"The phrase 'Joel Franklin residence' will not be easy for me to say," she said finally. "I hope you understand there will be a price for this service, Mr. Franklin."

I couldn't hear a smile in her voice, so I said, "You're a wonderful person?"

Georgie responded, "Nice try, buster, but you still owe me."

When I arrived home for lunch, Annie met me at the door and said, "You're mean, Daddy! Mommy and I are mad at you."

I could see Georgie standing behind her, smiling.

I said, "I'm sorry, princess, but it was an important call that Mommy had to answer."

Annie turned on her heel and stomped away.

"I take it you got the telephone call, then," I said to Georgie.

"I did. I had the privilege of speaking to the great Dr. Plimpton himself. He assumed I was your secretary," she added with a glare. "He informed me that he would be glad to meet you. He said it would be most convenient if you could attend his next séance in London. There's one Wednesday evening, June 14th, at 7:00 PM, at the Barbara Watkins's residence on Talbot Street North."

Georgie gave me an impish look and said, "It's an experience we should *both* enjoy."

"Uh, sure," I said, feeling there was no other possible answer under the circumstances.

After lunch, I retreated back to my desk at the police station. I had some paperwork to tidy up. That took me until almost two o'clock. Signing off the last form, I called Celeste Bedgegood and asked if I could interview her housekeeper, Sarah Olson, this afternoon.

"Come over now, if you like," Celeste answered. "Just don't take up too much of her time, I'm the one who's paying her."

I promised I wouldn't, but she'd already hung up.

Shortly after two thirty, Sarah and I were seated in Celeste's home office. Sarah was somewhat younger than Violet, perhaps in her late thirties, with dark blonde hair pinned up in a bun. She was wearing a patterned blue dress. Her hands were chapped and red.

Before I could start my interview, Sarah said, "We've got to make this quick, you know. I've got work to do, and I don't want to lose no pay because of some wasted time."

"This won't take long if you answer my questions honestly," I replied, used to this kind of surliness. Being interviewed by a detective made people nervous. "When you don't answer properly, I get suspicious, and I ask more questions, and then the interview lasts longer."

Sarah took the hint. "What's this all about?" she said. "Why do I need to be interviewed?"

"I was sent here by the chief of police—" I started.

"By 'chief' you mean her nephew, Lawrence?" she said.

"Yes, Chief Bedgegood," I said, concealing my irritation at the interruption. "Mrs. Bedgegood reported something stolen from her house."

"I didn't steal nothing," said Sarah. "Just because my husband was a criminal, doesn't mean I'm a criminal."

"No one said you were the thief, Sarah," I said. "No one has accused you of anything."

I saw a subtle change in her expression. "It's about the open window that I told Mrs. Bedgegood about, right? That proves I didn't steal nothing, or I wouldn't have told her about the window."

She was growing agitated, so I paused for a few seconds to let her calm down. Then I recommenced the interview.

"How long have you worked for Mrs. Bedgegood?" I asked.

"It'll be three years now, ever since me 'usband went to jail," she said with a smile. "Best thing that's happened to me in years."

"So, you're very happy working for Mrs. Bedgegood, then?"

"No, not at all," said Sarah, making a face. "She's a hard devil to please. 'Twas my husband going to jail that was the good thing. No bruises for three years," she said, showing me her bare, bruiseless arm. "He was just a layabout crook."

"What was he put in jail for?" I asked.

"It was like stealing—'twas fraud. He went around trying to steal money from old ninnies by selling them stuff that didn't exist. And if that didn't work, that way he got to know about their house and the best way to break in."

I felt a brief flicker of excitement. Sarah's husband would be an excellent suspect ... the only problem was that he'd been in jail for three years. Or had he?

"What's your husband's name?" I asked.

"Kenny. Kenny Olson. Or Kenneth. Or Ken. I don't know what they put him under at the jail. That's where you can find him."

I asked a few more questions for background information before I got to the important questions I wanted to ask.

"There was a séance here a couple weeks ago," I said. "Were you here that evening?"

Sarah gave me a puzzled look, thought for a minute, and said, "Do you mean that important meeting where Dr. Primrose came and talked to spirits?"

I nodded and asked, "What did you think of the meeting, Sarah?"

"Oh, it was malarkey. Entertainment, I suppose, for the old women. I've certainly drank lots of spirits but never enough so I saw spirits or talked to 'em," she said and laughed loudly.

She stopped laughing abruptly.

"Pardon me, sir, I don't mean to offend nobody. Thems as has it can spend it any fool way they want."

"I'm surprised you were at the house that night," I said. "You're not a cook. She wouldn't have needed your services."

"No, but I'm friends with Violet, and one of the other girls called in sick, and they needed some bodies to clean up afterwards."

I would have to get the name of the girl who called in sick.

"Were you in the kitchen a lot of the time while the séance was going on?"

"I was," she said. "It's where they needed the help."

"So, you could see down the main hall all the way to the front of the house."

"You can from the kitchen, yes."

"Did you see anybody come up the main hall and go into Mrs. Bedgegood's office? I mean the room we're sitting in now."

"I wasn't looking down the hall much," said Sarah. "But there was an older lady—I don't know her name—who walked down the hall before the séance ended." Sarah paused and then said, "Wait, that one nephew of hers, Kurtis somebody, he came in the back door and walked past us in the kitchen. Never so much as 'ello and then into this office. And now that I think about it, I don't remember him coming back out."

"Thank you for your time, Sarah. You gave me some very helpful information. I'll put in a good word for you with Mrs. Bedgegood."

"Thanks," she said, smiling. "Now I gotta get back to work. Idle hands, Detective."

Saturday, June 10th

As soon as lunch was finished on Saturday, Annie came up to me and said, "Daddy, you promised."

Uh-oh.

I couldn't very well say I'd forgotten what I had promised my daughter, so I looked at Georgie. Indulgently, she nodded and said, "It's okay, Annie, Daddy will be ready in a minute to take us to Danny's Diner and Ice Cream Parlour for that special treat he promised us yesterday after lunch."

Annie stood impatiently by the door while Mommy and Daddy got ready to leave.

We went out, following Annie, and got in into our Chevy sedan. As I pulled out of the driveway, Georgie said, "Remember, don't drive down any rough roads or hit any potholes. That wedding is next Saturday, and I don't want to miss it. Not only that, I have an exciting date this Wednesday night."

She gave me a wink.

Danny's wasn't busy yet, but I knew it would be packed with young people early this evening. Annie wanted to sit at the counter, but we told her the seats were too high and she'd have to wait until she was bigger. We sat at a table by the window instead. Annie got her favourite, a Neapolitan ice cream cone. Georgie decided on a chocolate marshmallow sundae, while I settled for a vanilla milkshake.

The sun was shining, everyone was happy, and we enjoyed our treat. A promise is a promise, and I'm glad I kept mine.

I spent the afternoon doing chores and helping Georgie around the house, then after supper the three of us gathered around the Philco radio in the living room. It was almost half past six, and Annie was looking forward to listening to *Let's Pretend*, which had been moved from its Saturday morning slot to an evening slot the previous year. On the last episode, they'd told the story of Cinderella, which Annie, naturally, found delightful. Tonight's episode was to be about Rumpelstiltskin. Annie loved the show, even though she was quite young. I think it was because of the child actors.

Fibber McGee and Molly, a comedy show about a husband and wife, came on at seven o'clock. Georgie didn't particularly care for the show, so it was a good time for her to get Annie ready for bed. I listened to Fibber verbally spar with Molly while I worked on our latest jigsaw puzzle.

Georgie and I both look forward to *The Jack Benny Program*, or *The Jello Program*, as it was currently called, which came on next, at seven thirty. The characters are ridiculous exaggerations of real people, but we have acquaintances that seem very similar to some of them. Our private joke when we're alone is to say, "I think"—and here we would insert a friend's name—"just did a Jack Benny."

We enjoyed tonight's show except, of course, for Jack attempting to play his violin. Once the show ended, at eight o'clock, Georgie said, "Are you going to try and contact Dora tonight?"

Georgie and I had talked earlier in the day, when Annie wasn't around, about contacting Dora.

We'd found out about Dora shortly after we'd moved into this house on Princess Ave., when Annie had begun talking about 'the nice lady.' Georgie and I had been mystified at first, but upon questioning it turned out that this mysterious woman, whom neither of us had ever seen, and who was talking to Annie, shared the house with us. Georgie and I quickly realized that Dora was a ghost, or essence, as I prefer to call them, and that Annie had inherited from me the ability to communicate with essences.

This communication isn't verbal and audible, though it most often takes the form of a conversation inside the mind. I believe that what my daughter and I are picking up on is some type of electromagnetic signal in a part of the spectrum that only certain people can receive and send. I don't know how many people have this ability, though I suspect it lies dormant in many. My own ability to communicate with essences didn't appear until after I'd been struck by lightning, when I was still a teenager living at home with my parents at 200 Durham Street in Chaseford. The sudden electrical discharge seemed to have activated some latent ability of mine. Since then, I have met a handful of other people with this same power. Annie's ability seems to have been active at birth.

There are conditions on the extent of this power. Only the essences of people who have died some kind of terrible or tragic death seem to be available for communication. These deaths are most often brutal and painful, or accompanied by a profound sense of betrayal. It's as if such essences cannot believe or accept what has happened to them and refuse to let go. Dora, as it turned out through investigations I had privately conducted, had been tortured to death in our very home on Princess Ave. by her deranged husband.

Dora and I have communicated occasionally since then. I wanted to make contact with her tonight because I wanted to be prepared for Wednesday night's séance. I was curious to find out if Dora knew anything about séances, and if spirits were really contacted at them.

Whenever possible, I had Georgie assist me while I communicated with essences. I would repeat out loud my questions and the responses I received while she took notes, so that we would have a written record of the communication for later reference. Important information was sometimes forgotten after a session and only turned up later while perusing our notes.

With Georgie sitting beside me, notebook in hand, I settled into my chair, closed my eyes, and cleared my mind. There was no magic to what I was doing, I simply had to filter out any distractions. I concentrated on Dora, mentally repeating her name.

Ordinarily, in order to establish contact with an essence, you have to focus your attention on something which has deep emotional relevance to them, such as the nature of their death or the face of a loved one. This creates a sort of electromagnetic 'bridge' between your mind and the essence. In Dora's case, this was no longer necessary. Dora and I had communicated frequently enough that focusing on her name was sufficient. She made contact with me almost immediately.

"Is Annie okay?" she asked promptly.

Annie was always Dora's primary concern. Essences seemed to exist in a world all their own, perhaps repeating an echo of their former existence, and though at times aware of things happening in our world, they easily lost track of time. Fortunately, they also occasionally made contact with other essences in their echo world, which meant they were sometimes privy to information inaccessible to the living in other ways. I had often taken advantage of this in my work as a detective.

"Yes, there is no urgent problem," I sent back, repeating the exchange for Georgie's benefit. "I'd just like some information, or would like to know whom I could contact for information, about séances."

"There have never been any séances in this house, or in the neighbourhood nearby, that I know of," Dora communicated, "but Marlo, whom I occasionally contact, told me about a séance once.

"Marlo laughed when he told me about it. He said the man in charge of the séance acted like he was really important and pretended to speak to somebody's relatives. But there were no spirits nearby except for Marlo. The man was making it all up.

"Marlo thought he'd have some fun with the man, but as hard as Marlo tried to contact him, he couldn't get through. Marlo tried to communicate with the other people there, but no one could hear him. Marlo said it was all just a hoax so the man could make some money."

"Thanks, Dora. That helps a lot."

I related the contents of the message to Georgie.

Now at least part of my curiosity had been satisfied. Séances, in themselves, did not create special conditions for communicating with essences. It still depended on the ability of the persons conducting—or attending—the séance to establish contact. Which meant that most séances were probably acts of self-deception ... or con games.

Georgie looked up from her notes and said, "So séances are malarkey, are they? Well, I'm still looking forward to participating in the séance on Wednesday night. I'm sure it will be fun."

Monday, June 12th

The first thing I did Monday morning was locate Kenny Olson. After a quick call to the London Jail, I confirmed that he was still being housed there. There was no way he could be responsible for the theft, so I crossed him off my list.

I turned next to my paperwork, catching up with the past week. Lucky for me—and my paperwork—Chief Bedgegood didn't call me into his office this morning, but he did drop by my desk.

"My aunt Celeste is going to drive me nuts," he grumbled. "We had her over to our place on Sunday. We do this from time to time; she seems to enjoy her visits with us, though you'd never know it while she was there.

"I asked my aunt how her interview went with you. She told me you were very nice young man, but she didn't know how competent a detective you were. She said you had a problem getting in the front door. I'm not sure what she meant, and I wasn't going to ask, but I'm assuming she forgot her ear trumpet and slammed the door in your face before you could say anything. She's done that to me on more than one occasion."

I nodded and said, "That's exactly what happened."

"Aunt Celeste told me that you interviewed the cook, Violet Murphy, and her housekeeper, Sarah Olson. Did you learn anything important from them?"

"Not really," I said, "but I have finagled an invitation to the next séance. It's on Wednesday night, at the residence of Barbara Watkins on Talbot Street North. Your aunt doesn't know yet, so please don't say anything."

"I won't say a word," said Bedgegood, "but that's a pretty fancy crowd you're keeping company with. Better wear something nice."

"Oh, it's you, Detective Franklin," said Sarah Olson that afternoon when she answered the door at Celeste Bedgegood's. She was obviously disappointed.

"You don't look happy to see me," I said.

"I was hopin' it was Connor McDougall," she said, holding up a basket covered with a cloth. "I have four fresh June muffins for Connor that Violet said I could have. Violet's been makin' muffins all morning. Ma'am is havin' some delivered to Barbara Watkins's house for the important séance meeting Wednesday night."

"What are June muffins?" I asked.

"That's just what Violet calls them," said Sarah, raising the cloth to show me the muffins. "To me they look like ordinary muffins with fresh berries in them."

I had to concur.

"I'm sorry I'm not Connor," I said. "The muffins look delicious. I came to see Mrs. Bedgegood, if she's in."

"She told me you'd likely be here sometime today to talk to Horace," Sarah said, covering the muffins. "Do you want me to have Horace come into the house?"

"Not yet. I'd like to speak to Mrs. Bedgegood first," I replied.

Celeste Bedgegood was sitting in her large drawing room with an embroidery kit and a half-finished project: a bouquet of flowers. She had her ear trumpet, and I knew she favoured her left ear, so I sat to that side of her.

She smiled at me, set aside her needlework, and said, "You have detective potential. You're observant, and you have a good memory. I see you've correctly deduced where to sit when having a conversation with me."

I smiled back and said, "I appreciate the compliment."

"I know you're likely here to see Horace," she said. "He's out in the garden right at the moment. What do you want of me?"

Putting on my most pleasant look, I said, "I have a favour to ask of you. As part of my investigation into the theft of your special British biscuit box and its contents."

Celeste gave me a stern look and said, "Tell me what you've done and what I need to do to help you."

There was no getting anything past Celeste.

"I've been invited to attend the séance on Wednesday evening at Barbara Watkins's house."

Celeste was obviously surprised. "Somehow, I think you must've taken my name in vain, Detective. I can't think of any other way you'd get invited to Barbara Watkins's house. Tell me the details."

I had been prepared for an inquisition, and it didn't seem I'd be disappointed. I told her about my call to Dr. Harold Plimpton's residence, and I told her about asking Georgie to answer the phone as if she were my receptionist. I also told her Georgie's response.

Celeste chortled delightedly and said, "I like your wife's attitude. You obviously need correction from time to time."

I was greatly relieved by her reaction. I feared it might be very difficult to get Celeste Bedgegood to allow me to accompany her to Barbara Watkins's séance.

"Would it be acceptable if my wife, who is extremely pregnant, accompanies us too?" I asked.

"Why, I'd be delighted," she said. "In fact, you'd better bring her along, or I might change my mind. You may accompany Georgie and me to the séance, Detective.

"Though I don't know why I put up with that Dr. Harold Plimpton," she continued, making a face. "He's such a pretentious ass. But this deception sounds like fun. I'm not convinced I believe in this kind of thing—spirits, the afterlife, divination—but séances *are* entertaining.

"I'll introduce you and Georgie as very close friends of the family. You and your wife need to be at my house by half past six. I'll have us driven over to the Watkins's house in a chauffeured limousine."

"Thank you. We'll be here," I said.

I got up to leave.

"Sit back down for a minute, young man," Celeste Bedgegood said, suddenly serious. "I'm going to tell you something else because I trust you. You didn't cut corners telling me about how you contacted Dr. Plimpton, so I'm going to tell you something not even my nephew, the chief, knows. I doubt if it has anything to do with the theft of the biscuit box, but you never know.

"Many years ago, my late husband's brother Elias Bedgegood got into extreme financial difficulty. He owned a large farm on the edge of town, but he made a series of very poor decisions and ended up owing an unsavoury man a lot of money.

The man threatened him and said that if he didn't pay up, he would be killed. Elias offered this villain his farm in payment, but he was told, 'I don't want your land, I want the money. Besides your farm's not worth what you owe me.'

"Elias came to my husband, Compton, and begged him to pay the man. My husband paid on the condition that his brother would transfer the ownership of his farm to Compton. My husband told him he would accept the farm as payment in full for covering Elias's debt, even though the money owed was for far more than double the value of the farm. Compton told his brother Elias that he and his family could continue to live on the farm as though nothing had happened. This was a secret between Compton and Elias; Elias's wife and family knew nothing about the near tragedy that Compton had saved them from.

"Compton personally paid the debt and had the recipient give him a receipt. Among the documents the stolen British biscuit box contained was that receipt and a letter written by Elias explaining the situation and thanking Compton for his generous help."

I let her story sink in. Celeste Bedgegood watched me carefully.

"So there's a possibility that someone stole the British biscuit box because it contained documents relevant to the situation you just described," I said.

She nodded, "That's one possibility. But there is also a small fortune in bearer bonds in the box. I just thought you should have all the information."

I thanked her again and excused myself. She had given me much to think about as I walked down the main hall to her office. As I passed Sarah Olson, I asked her if she would call Horace Walker in from his yard work.

I was barely seated behind the desk when a tall, angular man in his mid-fifties appeared. "You must be Horace," I said.

He nodded and said, "I guess you have questions I have to answer. I don't have a lot of time; I've got a man out there in the yard helping me this morning. He doesn't always know what to do next. And he doesn't always ask for instructions."

"It won't take long," I said. "Please have a seat."

Horace seated himself, careful not to get dirt on the chair.

"He's a good sort," Horace resumed. "He's kinda sweet on that Sarah woman. But he'd best be careful. He's lucky he didn't get locked up along with her husband, who is not a good sort."

"By any chance, is your man Connor McDougall?" I asked, instantly alert.

"'Tis," said Walker.

"How does Connor know Kenny Olson?"

"I don't know," Horace said with a shrug. "I guess they were friends."

I took out my notepad and added Connor McDougall's name to the list of people I should interview.

The interview with Horace went quickly. He didn't have a lot to say. He had worked for Mrs. Bedgegood and her husband for over twenty years, and they had always treated him fairly. He said he rarely came in the house, and he knew nothing about séances.

Tuesday, June 13th

At suppertime yesterday, I told Georgie that Celeste Bedgegood was delighted to have us attend the séance with her. Since then, Georgie has been on the telephone trying to locate, as she described it to me, 'Proper formal wear for the occasion.'

She was on the phone all evening. When I was on my way out the door for the police station this morning, she was still on the telephone. I told her not to worry, I could just wear my 'go to church' clothes. She frowned at me and said in a daunting voice, "You have no idea."

Georgie then reminded me that we also had an important social engagement on Saturday. It took a moment to register, but when it did, I came to a full stop. I had been so caught up in my new case that I had almost forgotten about the wedding of our friends Dr. Alfred Khryscoff and Gwen Cummings this Saturday.

"Go to work, Joel, you'll be late. And you're distracting me," said Georgie, dialing another number.

Going to work suddenly did seem like a good idea. Finding a missing biscuit box seemed much easier than finding something to wear for a fancy social outing.

Before I left Celeste Bedgegood's home on Central Ave. yesterday, I'd obtained from her the telephone number of her nephew Kurtis Donnelly. Kurtis was the only son of Elias Bedgegood. Violet Murphy, the cook, had seen him in the house the night of the séance, which put him at the scene of the crime. I also got the number of the girl who'd been away sick, though it was probably a dead end.

I called Mr. Donnelly last night and arranged an interview with him at his home on Emery Street in south London at seven o'clock tonight. I was going to spend the day in the office, organizing the information that I'd collected so far on the theft of the British biscuit box and valuable documents from Celeste Bedgegood. I asked Constable Brian Carmichael to follow up with the sick girl. I'd worked with Carmichael a number of times and had great respect for his abilities. He was determined to become a detective, and I trusted him to sniff out any potential leads.

I started by listing potential suspects. I didn't have enough information to have a prime suspect, but I had some people that I thought were worth investigating further. In my notebook, I jotted:

- Kurtis Donnelly, Celeste's nephew

- Sarah Olson, housekeeper (husband, Kenny, is a known felon who has been in jail for the past three years)

- Connor McDougall, Horace Walker's assistant, friend of Sarah and Kenny

- Dr. Harold Plimpton, conducts séances; could be involved in a confidence scam

As a detective, I had learned the hard way that sometimes the people you suspect of being guilty aren't, and that someone on the periphery of your investigation turns out to be the guilty party.

So I had another list of names that included:

- Violet Murphy, cook
- Girl who called in sick the night of the séance
- Horace Walker, gardener
- Dr. Plimpton's assistants
- Ladies involved in the séance at Celeste's
- Chief Bedgegood

Owing to the last name on this list, I kept the second list hidden in my coat pocket.

Emery Street was a far different type of neighbourhood than the one Celeste Bedgegood resided in. Kurtis Donnelly lived in a one-storey Ontario cottage that had seen better days. The paint on the bricks was peeling, the grass on the lawn was too long, and the shrubs were all overgrown. A lot of the nearby homes had a similar, rundown appearance. But it was a lively neighbourhood; there were lots of kids and dogs running around, as well as a couple of chickens. There was much shouting, laughing, and barking. Right now, there was a game of baseball going on in the middle of the street, and I had to slow down to avoid running over the third baseman.

I manoeuvred my way into the Donnelly driveway, weaving around a bicycle that was lying on the edge of the lane, and parked behind an older Chevy. I checked the time on my watch; it was seven o'clock. When I knocked on the front door of the house, a short, stocky man about fifty or so years of age appeared. He had a world-weary look about him, and his clothes looked like they could have used a good wash.

I introduced myself.

The man nodded. "Come on in," he said, "I'm Kurtis."

We entered his home, which smelled strongly of baked beans. I was immediately in the cramped living room, where I met Sally, Kurtis's wife, two young daughters, and their two cats. Sally, who appeared to be about fifteen years younger than Kurtis, greeted me a little apprehensively. After shaking my hand, she rounded up the children and left the room so Kurtis and I could have some privacy.

"Would you like a Labatt's, Det. Franklin?" Kurtis asked me with a good-humoured grin.

"Wish I could," I said, "but no thanks."

"Not on the job, right?" he said, disappearing into the next room, which I surmised was the kitchen.

"That's right."

I heard him rummaging around and bottles clinking.

"I was really surprised when you called and told me something had been stolen from Aunt Celeste's," Kurtis said, returning with an open green bottle. "I usually get along well with my aunt, and I was kind of hurt that I had to be interviewed. But my wife, Sally, she said, 'The police have to interview anyone who was in or near the house the night of the theft. It's part of their procedure.' After thinking about it, I guess it makes sense. So no hard feelings, Detective. Just move that stuff out of the way and sit down."

I moved a pile of raggedy dolls and some blankets aside and sat down on the threadbare sofa. I took my notepad and pencil out of my pocket.

Kurtis seemed relaxed, so I proceeded with my questions. When I'd completed my introductory questioning, I moved on to something that had puzzled me.

"Your father was Mr. Bedgegood's brother. I believe his name was Elias Bedgegood. I noticed that your last name is not Bedgegood. Do you mind telling me the reason behind that?"

Kurtis was no longer relaxed; the muscles on his face had tightened, and I could see anger in his eyes. He took a sip of his beer, swallowing hard.

"I do mind," he muttered, "but it's probably better for me to tell you than for you to get the information from someone else. Someone who may be biased.

"Most boys look up to their father, but my father was a weak man, Detective, and his stupidity cost me my inheritance and upset my mother a great deal. A year or so before he died, my father told me that he didn't own the farm.

"I was shocked, I was angry, and I was upset. It was our home. Where were we going to live when he died? I didn't have a lot of respect for my father before he told me, and I sure didn't have any after. I decided to change my name to my mother's maiden name. I was so angry, I didn't want any reminders. I didn't even want to think of my father.

"It was a bad time for me, Detective. I lashed out at everyone. I went to see my uncle and threatened to sue him for taking advantage of my father."

Kurtis stopped for a moment and put his head in his hands. Finally, he sighed and looked up.

"My uncle was very patient with me," he continued. "After some of the things I said, he had every right to decide to never see me again. But about two weeks after my father died, my uncle asked me to come over for a visit. He and Aunt Celeste sat with me and showed me the receipt for the money that my dad owed, and showed me the agreement letter my father signed that transferred the farm to him as payment for my uncle Compton covering the debt.

"Aunt Celeste has always treated me well. She told me I was welcome to come and go as I please at their house. She had no children of her own and has always treated her nephews and nieces in a kind and generous manner."

Kurtis Donnelly had run out of the steam. He seemed distracted and possibly a little drunk.

We sat there for a few minutes in silence while I jotted down a couple of notes and Kurtis nursed his beer.

Finally, I said, "Kurtis, you were at your aunt's house the night of the séance. Sarah Olson, your aunt's housekeeper, said you came in the back door and went through the kitchen, and then went into your aunt's office. Why did you go in there?"

"My youngest girl, Stella, left her doll there," he said, gesturing toward the pile of dolls I'd moved aside. "We'd visited my aunt Celeste the day before the séance, and Stella—she's seven—had taken her favourite doll with her to show her great aunt. She forgot it. Aunt Celeste told me I could pick the doll up after I finished work. She'd leave it in her office because, by the time I came over, the séance would likely be in progress."

"What did you notice when you went in the office?" I asked.

"I was surprised," Kurtis said. "There was an older woman in the office, sitting in a chair. At first, I thought I was seeing a ghost." He chuckled. "She seemed to be sleeping, and I didn't want to disturb her, so I just grabbed the doll and left. The other thing that struck me as a little strange was that the window was wide open. But I figured the woman just wanted some fresh air."

"What door did you leave by?"

"There's a door right beside the office door, just before you get to the kitchen. That door opens to a small landing. You go down about half a dozen steps, and then you can either turn and go down some more steps to the basement, or you can go straight ahead out the side door. I went out that side door. The gardener, Horace Walker, uses that door all the time."

We talked for a few more minutes, and the conversation wandered onto other subjects. I told him my wife was expecting, and that I had little girl, Annie, almost three years old. He told me he and his wife, Sally, had four kids. The two older children, Kurtis Jr. and Susan, were no longer living at home, but Kitty and Stella were still in school.

"They're great until they're teenagers," he said with a chuckle.

I thanked him for his cooperation and returned to the police station. On my desk, I found a report from Cst. Carmichael. It was about the sick girl. She'd been at home with her mother and sister and could provide a doctor's note if required. In his opinion, she didn't seem suspicious. I crossed her name off my list.

It was almost nine o'clock by the time I got home to Princess Ave. Georgie met me at the door with an excited gleam in her eye.

"I did it, I did it!" she exclaimed.

It was now my turn to say, "What did you do?"

"Do you know Gerry's friend Rosalyn?" she asked.

I didn't know Gerry, so therefore I didn't know Rosalyn, so I said, "No, I can't place her."

"Gerry was Tabitha's best friend," said Georgie, identifying this as the source of my confusion. "She went to our school, but she's a year older than you. Do you remember that, before my brother, Robert, went to England, he was friends for a long time with Tabitha? My mother thought he and Tabitha might get married. It didn't happen. I think Gerry had something to do with that. Anyway, that's ancient history."

I looked at her, more bewildered than ever, but trusting that all would be made clear in time.

"It turns out that when Gerry was going to school in Toronto, she met Rosalyn," Georgie continued. "Roslyn has a cousin Becky who is quite wealthy, and Becky knows a woman who owns a high-end fashion store in Burlington; so, as luck would have it, while I was making a number of phone calls late this morning—I stopped to make some coffee, which was lucky because the woman in Burlington, Becky's friend, got back to me and said, because Roslyn was such a good friend of mine—that's an exaggeration, I really don't know Rosalyn that well—but anyway, because Roz is such a good friend of mine, she would send formal wear for both of us, even though I'm quite pregnant. She said she would send it to us gratis, but we would have to have it cleaned and returned in mint condition. I thanked her profusely. I am so delighted because now we will be dressed properly for the occasion."

I thought—prayed, rather—this was the end of her narrative and opened my mouth to reply. Prematurely, as it turned out.

"When I said that you were busy working on a special investigation for the chief of police," Georgie continued, "the woman that owns the store was so excited to learn that you were a famous detective that she said she would make arrangements to have our garments delivered to us. It turns out that her brother is a friend of the son of the mayor of London, and he was coming to London this afternoon. So, you will not believe this, but a couple of simple telephone calls and our huge clothing problem was solved. They arrived this afternoon, and the outfits are wonderful! I tried mine on. It's a gorgeous gown. It's the most marvelous shade of purple. It's like a dream. I've looked at your suit, and it's amazing! We're so lucky!"

She wrapped her arms around my neck and hugged me almost off of my feet.

I hadn't seen Georgie this excited since our wedding. And though I couldn't follow half the connections she'd made to get the stuff, I had to agree we were really lucky. Though I certainly wasn't going to call what she'd put so much effort into getting 'stuff.'

Wednesday, June 14th

Georgie was shaking me.

I jerked my head up off the pillow, looking around blearily. Sunlight was just beginning to creep in through the window. "What's going on?" I asked, still groggy. I looked at the alarm clock on the nightstand. It was just after 6:00 AM. We didn't usually get up until 6:30. "It's early."

"You were having a bad dream," said Georgie. "You were shouting, so I woke you up."

"Shouting? Shouting what?" I said, sitting up. Fragments of a dream were teasing at the edge of my awareness but refused to come into focus.

"You were saying, 'I don't know, I don't know,' and 'Who are you people?' You seemed to be getting very upset, so I thought I'd better wake you. I didn't want you to kick me."

Georgie was right to be concerned. I'd given her a pretty solid whack a few years ago when I'd been having nightmares about Thessalus Redd, the delusional killer who'd carved his path of blood across Canada. Unlike most people, who had the good sense to stay still when they were sleeping, I had a tendency to act out my dreams.

"I'm okay now," I said, rubbing my eyes. The dream was coming back to me now. "It wasn't even a nightmare, just a very frustrating dream. I was at a reunion of some kind, and I'd been introduced to my friend's half-brother's cousin's second wife's sister's son-in-law's best friend's son."

"I suppose that could be confusing," Georgie said, "especially if you weren't paying attention. Come to think of it, I think that actually happened, Joel, when we were at a reunion on your dad's side. Don't you recall? The boy's name was Marvin."

"Vaguely," I said, having no wish to remember. Unlike an old colleague of mine from Chaseford, Cst. Jake Smith, who was fond of delineating arcane family relationships, I really wanted no part of this conversation.

Georgie could tell. "Okay, Mr. Grumpy Gus," she said, "Let's change the subject. I'll put on my beautiful new evening gown. I've been waiting since yesterday to show you."

She hopped off the bed and disappeared into the closet. A couple of minutes later, she returned in a shimmering purple gown. Standing in the fresh morning sunlight, with her auburn hair hanging down over her shoulders, she looked simply ravishing. You could hardly tell that she was nine months pregnant.

"You look amazing," I said, jumping off the bed to embrace her. "That is a gorgeous dress on a gorgeous woman."

"Take it easy, buster," she said, giggling. "You've got to get to work."

"I will. In a minute..."

I looked up from my report and glared at the clock. I was impatient for the day to be over. I wanted it to pass quickly so I could get to the séance; at the same time, I had to remember that I had given myself a role to play. I knew Georgie would love showing off her dazzling new evening dress, but I was a little apprehensive as to what to expect at Barbara Watkins's. I knew a fair bit about dealing with essences, and I was about ninety-nine percent certain the séance was a piece of theatre and not a real communion with the spirit world, but it was that one percent that bothered me. What if I *did* make contact with an essence during the séance? It could be very awkward with so many people around.

Finally, the day was over. I went directly home, and Georgie and I got ready. Our neighbour Kay Dunnigan came over while we were getting dressed to look after Annie. When we came downstairs, Annie said, "You look like a princess, Mommy!"

"And what do I look like?" I said.

"You look like Daddy!" said Annie.

Georgie and Kay both laughed.

"You look like a proper gentleman," said Auntie Kay.

"I suppose that beats looking like a waiter," I said, inspecting my cuffs.

Georgie gave me a look that told me it was time for us to go. Auntie Kay and Annie waved us goodbye as we left.

We were about ten minutes early getting to Celeste Bedgegood's residence on Central Ave. I banged the stern, matronly door knocker and warned Georgie not to be surprised if there was a kerfuffle, relating my prior experience of Celeste answering the door without her ear trumpet.

We were lucky; the door was answered by Sarah Olson, the housekeeper. She recognized me immediately and, turning to Georgie, said, "This must be your amazin' wife."

I introduced them and Sarah said, "Pleased to meet ya," with something like a curtsey. She looked Georgie up and down with visible envy and added, "That's a wonderful evenin' dress, ma'am."

Celeste must've heard the commotion at the door for she was there within the minute, ear trumpet in hand. After more introductions, she said, "Heavenly days, Georgie, you look wonderful. Like one of the Greek muses. You certainly don't look like a mother-to-be in waiting. My friends will be thrilled to meet you." She turned to me and said, "The guy in the tuxedo with you looks okay too."

"Thank you," said Georgie. "A compliment is never amiss with me, but don't say too many nice things to Joel, he'll just get carried away."

They both laughed.

I smiled and said, "I can handle anything but a compliment. I'm as tough as—"

"A marshmallow," said Georgie, and she and Celeste both laughed again.

I chose the better part of valour and remained silent.

Just then, a large, sleek, black Lincoln Model K limousine pulled up in front of the house.

"Here's Paul," said Celeste.

"Perfect," said Georgie, eyes widening in appreciation for the magnificent vehicle.

"Shall we?" said Celeste, leading us down to the limousine as Paul got out to open the doors.

"Be careful," he said as we all climbed in. "I borrowed this from a friend."

Paul appeared to be in his seventies, a tall man with white hair who was still in good health. He must have been quite impressive when he was younger. Paul was polite and quiet and drove very carefully.

Twenty minutes later, just before seven o'clock, we pulled up in front of Barbara Watkins's English manor on Talbot Street North. It was an impressive and somewhat imposing grey stone structure, and one of the biggest homes I'd ever seen.

As I reached for the door handle to get out, Celeste slapped my hand and pointed at the doorman approaching the car. "He'll open the door," she said.

The doorman escorted the three of us across the flagstone, under the portico, to the open front door, where we were met by a man in a tailcoat, waistcoat, and bowtie, who I assumed was the butler. The butler led us through the foyer to a pair of double doors opening onto a large, brilliantly lit, but somewhat oddly structured drawing room.

The drawing room was forty feet long, thirty feet wide, and had twelve-foot ceilings. One wall was dominated by high windows. In the centre of the room was a polygonal wooden enclosure about fifteen feet in diameter and twelve feet high. Above this unusual structure was a gas chandelier. Lining the inner walls of the main room were a number of comfortable chairs and small tables, arranged tastefully below what I was sure were quite valuable paintings.

The butler announced us to the small crowd gathered within: "Mrs. Celeste Bedgegood and her good friends Georgina and Joel Franklin."

A group of five elderly women and two old men immediately turned to see who had arrived. Within seconds, Georgie was surrounded by the pack of old ladies ooing and ahhing her dress, while I was left to shake hands with two men twenty years older than my father, Edward Chavin and Arthur Brightman. A younger couple, closer to our own age, who had arrived with three children ranging in age from about four to eleven, remained off to one side, having an animated discussion about the propriety of stuffing one's cheeks with pastries. A waiter came around with a tray of drinks, but I declined. I needed my wits about me.

After we had all chatted for about five minutes, a tall, distinguished-looking gentleman about fifty-five years of age, wearing pince-nez and sporting a moustache, approached me and introduced himself as Dr. Harold Plimpton, one of the few world experts on thaumaturgy.

"It's a pleasure to meet you, Doctor," I said, falling into my role nicely. "Your understanding of the spirit world, and your appreciation of the miraculous, has not gone unnoticed by me or my influential friends."

I was amazed at how easily this claptrap slipped from my tongue.

To the great Dr. Plimpton my words must have seemed apropos and heartfelt, for he immediately produced a bright smile and a firm handclasp and said, "I've been looking forward to meeting you, Mr. Franklin."

Knowing he couldn't possibly have known anything about me, I almost responded, "Huh?" but under the stern eye of my coach, Georgie, I said, "The pleasure is all mine."

My bluff rated a brief introduction to Plimpton's two very solemn assistants, Simon and Simone, who appeared to be twins. They were of average height and average appearance, and because they were wearing uniforms, it was hard to tell them apart, except that her hair was longer than his. They appeared to be in their early forties. They didn't say much.

Dr. Plimpton checked the time on his gold watch, clapped his hands together twice, and in a loud voice announced, "We must now retire to the séance area!"

The séance area, it turned out, was the odd little enclosure in the centre of the drawing room. The drawing room, which housed the séance area, was a beautiful room, carefully decorated to impress friends, but much too large for the intimate setting required for a séance.

As we filed into the little chamber, Celeste informed me that Barbara had commissioned a renowned local artisan to construct it, including the eight beautiful panels, which were six feet wide and ten feet tall. Each panel was painted a different, soothing pastel colour on the inside of the chamber. The panels had been inserted into a framework of oak supports with a solid base, creating a large octagon. One panel was hinged and served as a door to the inner chamber. The simplicity and beauty of this octagonal room produced a temple-like setting.

In the centre of the room was an octagonal table. The sides of this table were parallel to the sides of the surrounding octagon. I was the only male to be chosen to sit with the seven ladies. The two older men, and the younger couple with three children, had to content themselves by sitting in the outer area of the drawing room. As the octagon had no ceiling, they would be able to hear what was going on in the séance but would not be active participants.

Dr. Plimpton asked us to sit around the octagonal table and took his place behind an ornate pulpit next to the wall opposite the door. There was a small antique table beside the pulpit. A golden cloth was draped over the table, and a Ouija board and a planchette had been carefully placed on the cloth.

Dr. Plimpton thanked Mrs. Watkins for the wonderful setting that she had provided for us. "This is a very special séance," he said. "It's important to remember that this chamber is a symbol of eternal life. You are seated at an octagon within an octagon, the optimal arrangement for a successful, meaningful, and spiritual experience.

"You will notice that in front of each of you there is a white candle," Dr. Plimpton continued. "These candles, signifying the destruction of negative energy and the arrival of peace, truth, and purity, will be lit by my assistants using a purple candle, which is symbolic of spiritual awareness, wisdom, and tranquility."

Dr. Plimpton clapped his hands sharply twice and his two assistants entered through the opening. Simon gracefully carried a golden tray, which held a single golden candleholder bearing a purple candle with a steady flame. When they reached the table, Simone took the handle of the candleholder and walked around the table, carefully lighting each of the eight white candles. When she was finished, she placed the golden candleholder back on the tray that Simon held, and they both exited the chamber. As they went through the door, all the exterior lights went out, including the great chandelier overhead. We were suddenly plunged into near darkness, our figures casting weird shadows in the flickering candlelight, petitioners in an octagonal temple awaiting the spirits.

For several moments, there was absolute silence, then Dr. Plimpton intoned, "Please join hands to demonstrate our unity of purpose and our common desire to communicate with the spiritual world."

I took the hand of Georgie, who was sitting to my right, and the hand of Celeste, who was sitting to my left. Despite my skepticism—not of the spirit world, but of Dr. Plimpton's abilities—I could feel the hairs on the back of my neck rise and my heartbeat increase. I could tell that Georgie and Celeste, too, had fallen under the spell cast by Dr. Plimpton.

Next, using his oratorical voice, Dr. Plimpton offered a prayer to the spirits, invoking them to accept our humble plea to join them. He paused and waited. Within seconds, several of the candles flickered. The result was a few startled 'ohs' from around the table. I was less impressed. It was nothing that couldn't have been caused by a draft from an open window. I closed my eyes and concentrated. I didn't detect the presence of an essence, but I also didn't know whom I would detect or how to make contact with them.

"We have now established the proper conditions for communication," Dr. Plimpton said in a reverent voice. "We will use a Ouija board and a planchette as our tools to communicate with the spirits. I will ask each of you in turn if you have a question. At that time, you may either ask your question or rap on the table twice if you have no question."

Dr. Plimpton called the first name, "Alice Mulder."

The woman named Alice shut her eyes and said, "Bernice, are you ... happy?"

Simone suddenly appeared at Alice's side, placing the Ouija board and planchette in front of her. Alice let go of her neighbours' hands and placed her own hands, one over the other, on top of the planchette. The women sitting to either side of Alice placed their hands on her shoulders. There was a moment of silence, during which we all—even I—held our breath. Then, as I watched from across the table, I saw the planchette slowly moving. It crept across the board with a dull scratching sound until it hovered over the word YES. Alice uttered a little gasp and started to weep, her shoulders gently trembling.

There was a pause for a moment or two while we waited for Alice to regain her composure, then Dr. Plimpton said, "Marian McKelvie."

The woman named Marian rapped the table twice.

"Celeste Bedgegood," Dr. Plimpton intoned.

Simone retrieved the board and planchette and placed it in front of Celeste. Somewhat awkwardly, I placed my hand on Celeste's shoulder. Celeste placed her hands on the planchette.

"Who's the thief?" Celeste demanded in the same tone I imagined she used when addressing her household staff.

The room had been very quiet up until now, but now there was a tomb-like silence. Even the whispering of the family and gentlemen outside the octagon ceased. Everyone, including myself and Dr. Plimpton, was astounded by her question.

Suddenly, there was a scream from outside the octagonal room. "He's dead! He's dead!" a woman cried.

Before we could respond, our little chamber erupted in chaos. The air was filled with hair-raising growls and snarls, as if a big cat, a lion or a tiger, had suddenly landed in the middle of our table, and small, brilliant, flashing lights began zipping and swerving over our heads. The candles, board, and planchette were flung from the table in all directions to clatter against the octagon walls.

The women were screaming. Even Georgie, who was not easily shaken, let out a high-pitched squeal. Dr. Plimpton and his assistants cowered behind the pulpit, covering their heads with their hands. I wrapped my arms around Georgie and Celeste and pulled them down under the table, trying to shield them with my body. The pandemonium continued for several minutes, then, as suddenly as it had begun, it ceased. There was a moment of absolute silence, and then I heard feet moving rapidly outside the chamber and the lights came back on. I could hear the crying of several young children.

I took Georgie's hand and helped her to her feet.

"Are you alright?" I said, more than a little shaken.

"I think so," she said, shivering and holding her belly. "That was a close one."

"Celeste?" I said, turning to Bedgegood's aunt.

"I didn't get my answer, but I sure got my money's worth," she said, rising to her feet, frazzled but stoic.

I led Georgie and Celeste through the door of the octagonal room back into the drawing room, where a small crowd was gathered about a person lying face up on the floor. The butler and one of his aides were kneeling beside the supine figure of Mr. Chavin, apparently trying to revive him. Mr. Brightman was standing behind them, shouting instructions and urging them on. The younger man was standing with them, looking pale and stunned, his wife off to one side, having drawn the children away to calm them and shield them from view of the fallen man.

Georgie went to assist the younger woman with her children, while Celeste marched boldly over to the cluster of men. I looked for Dr. Plimpton and found him standing dazed amid the mess in the séance room. He was too disoriented to be of any use, so I grabbed Simon and Simone and told them to see to the other women in the chamber, then went over to where Mr. Chavin lay.

Mr. Chavin was staring up at the ceiling with an expression of surprise and confusion on his face. His skin was a gruesome shade of red, and there was foam trickling down from the corners of his mouth. I didn't need a coroner to tell me he was no longer with us in the land of the living. My immediate assumption was that he'd died of a heart attack.

"Did anyone see what happened?" I asked the assembled men.

"You mean the lights?" said Mr. Brightman, turning to me. "Who could have missed it? It was like Ypres all over again!"

"No, not the lights. Mr. Chavin," I said, pointing at the body.

"Florence saw it," said the younger man in a weak voice. "That's my wife. She's over there with the children."

"Who are you?" I asked him.

"Neville. Neville Watkins. Barabara's my mother."

Before I could continue the investigation, two constables appeared in the drawing room. Csts. Carmichael and Johnson had arrived in answer to a frantic phone call from the Barbara Watkins's mansion.

"Hello, sir," said Cst. Carmichael, surprised to see me there, and even more surprised to see me in a tuxedo. "You seem to have beaten us to the scene. It looks a bit chaotic."

"It was pandemonium, briefly," I said. "Did you happen to notice anyone leaving when you arrived?"

"No sir," said Carmichael.

"That's good. I don't want anyone leaving," I said. "I don't think it's a crime scene, but we won't know for certain until the coroner arrives. I'll handle the group in here. I'd like you two to check the house and notify all staff that they can't leave until they have our permission."

"Yes sir," said Carmichael.

"Excuse me," said Mr. Brightman. "Did you say no one was allowed to leave?"

"That's right," I said.

"Are you in charge here?" he queried.

"I am. I'm a detective with the London Police."

"Well, then, Detective, you'd better send your men after Dr. Plimpton. I just saw him leaving with his assistants."

"Where?" I said with a touch of panic.

"Through the door," he said, pointing.

I nodded to Carmichael and the two constables hurried after them.

I crossed the room to where Barbara Watkins was sitting. Her eyes were red from crying, but she'd calmed down. She had her arms around another older woman, trying to comfort her.

"Please pardon the interruption," I said as gently as I could. "I should tell you that, not only am I a friend of Celeste's, but I'm also with the London Police Force."

"Thank goodness," said Barbara. "Maybe you can make sense of things. What's happening?"

"That's what I'm going to find out," I said.

The woman in her arms burst out in a fresh round of sobbing.

"This is Irma," said Barbara. "It was her husband, Edward, that died."

I introduced myself to Irma, but she was too distraught to do more than nod her head, blowing her nose on a handkerchief as she did so.

Another of the elderly women approached to offer her condolences. Barbara introduced us.

"Martha Brightman, this is Joel Franklin. He's with the police."

"You're Georgie's husband," said Martha. "I've heard all about you. I wish we could have met under better circumstances. I believe you've spoken to my husband, Arthur."

I indicated I had.

"And it was such a wonderful evening too, until those lights and noises started," Martha continued. "I'll never forget those sounds as long as I live. I've never been so terrified in my life! And then poor Edward dying all of a sudden in your drawing room, Barbara. It's terrible, simply unbearable! How could it have happened?"

Irma burst into a fresh round of tears. "Oh how? Why my Poor Edward? Why?" she cried.

"I hope to make some sense out of it for all of you," I said. "That man there, Neville, is your son?" I said to Barbara, turning and pointing where I thought he was only to find out that he was no longer there. I looked around and spied him leading his wife and children through a door. Georgie was with them.

"Yes. He's here with his wife, Florence, and their children," she said, nodding in their direction. "A séance isn't really the place for children—it was just supposed to be us and a couple of friends—but they arrived unexpectedly. I didn't think there would be any problem, so I let them stay. I couldn't have predicted..."

"Of course not," I said sympathetically. "Will you ladies excuse me for a moment?"

I could feel the situation spiralling out of control. First Plimpton and the twins, now Neville and his family. I couldn't keep my eye on everyone at the same time. If I didn't move fast, I could lose a valuable witness, to say nothing of a potential suspect.

I hurried through the door and found the Watkinses in a small sitting room. Neville was trying to reassure the children while Georgie and Florence talked.

"Excuse me," I said, interrupting the women. "My name's Joel, I'm a detective. Could I have a word with you, Florence?"

"Of course," said Florence. "Georgie told me you'd want to speak to me."

Unfortunately, Florence couldn't tell me anything of substance. She had seen Mr. Chavin fall from his chair, and when she'd gone to help him up, she'd realized he was dead.

Just then, Cst. Carmichael appeared at the door. I excused myself again and followed him into the drawing room.

"We caught Plimpton and his assistants in the lane. They were making a getaway in their 1939 Bentley," he said. "Fortunately, we'd blocked the lane when we came in, so they couldn't get out."

"Fleeing the scene?" I asked.

"Fleeing bad publicity is my guess," said the constable. "He kept asking us if we knew how it would look if word got around that someone had died at one of his séances. Cst. Johnson is keeping an eye on them." He looked over toward the séance chamber, where Johnson stood guard at the door. Dr. Plimpton and his assistants were once again ensconced safely within.

A few minutes later, the coroner, Dick Robinson, arrived. He stopped and looked at the wooden octagon, looked at the doctor of thaumaturgy and his assistants framed in the doorway, then looked around the room until he spotted me. He came over and said, "What's going on here, Joel? It's the first time I've ever seen a room inside a room."

"That's the séance chamber," I said.

"The séance chamber?" he repeated, bemused.

"Yes. I was in that chamber, taking part in the séance, when it happened."

"And what did happen?" he asked, looking down at the dead man.

"We heard someone shout, 'He's dead!' and when I came out, this older gentleman was on the floor right where you see him," I said. "They tried to revive him, but no one's moved him."

"Just like that, eh?" he said.

Dick approached the inert form of the old gentleman, looked him over, and then got down on his knees for a closer examination. After a few seconds, Dick stood up and came over to me.

"I hope you don't have plans for the rest the evening," he said. "He's dead, and I'm ninety-eight percent certain he died from cyanide poisoning. I'm certain the autopsy will confirm my hypothesis based on the brick-red hypostasis."

My confusion must have been obvious.

"Sorry, I'm speaking medicalese," said Dick. "I mean I predict it was cyanide based on the particular colour of his skin.

"Some of these other older people don't look too well either," he added, looking around. "I think you should have a doctor here, before we have anyone else lying on the floor."

I signaled for Barbara to come over so I could talk to her privately.

"It's not very good news," I said. "The coroner feels that the death of Mr. Chavin is suspicious. That means there will be a delay before people can leave. We will have to conduct brief interviews with everyone currently on the property. I'm sorry for the delay. I know it will upset many people. Your staff may be able to help us out by providing refreshments once I complete my announcement."

Mrs. Watkins nodded and said, "I'm upset myself, but I understand. You need to collect as much information as you can. We'll have to make the best of it. I'll talk to the staff. Is there anything else you need?"

"The coroner also noticed many of the older people look unwell," I replied. "He suggested that we have a doctor come."

"I'll call my personal physician, Dr. Smith," Mrs. Watkins said.

"Your cooperation is much appreciated," I said. "Could you make certain that everyone who was in the house at the time of these events, whether they're staff or friends or relatives, are together here in the drawing room for my announcement?"

"At once, Inspector."

I was pleased with the temporary promotion and—to avoid confusion—did not correct her.

I called Cst. Carmichael over and introduced him to Mrs. Watkins.

"I've just found out that the death was suspicious. I'll keep an eye on Plimpton. I want you and Johnson to round up everyone else who was on the property at the time of Mr. Chavin's death. Mrs. Watkins will tell you where to locate her staff and guests." I turned to Barbara Watkins and said, "When everyone is assembled, I need you to take a good look to make certain no one is missing."

"I'll be glad to do that, Inspector," she said.

Within fifteen minutes the drawing room was full. The staff had been assembled. It included the housekeeper and two maids, the cook and her three assistants, the butler and his two aides, six chauffeurs—including Paul—who'd been playing cards in the garage, the gardener, the handyman, and a nurse.

The others present included the seven women from the séance room, Celeste, Georgie, and the five older ladies, Barbara, Irma, Martha, Alice, and Marian, whom I hadn't yet met; Dr. Plimpton and his assistants, Simon and Simone; Mr. Brightman, Martha's husband; and Barbara Watkins's son Neville, his wife, Florence, and their three children. Thirty-five, in total. Not counting myself, the coroner, and the two constables. Or Mr. Chavin, of course, who was now discretely covered with a tablecloth.

I asked Barbara to come over and take inventory. She took a look at the entire group, paused, and said, "The only one missing is my invalid sister, Edith, who is bedridden. She has a small suite at the back of the second floor. I see that her nurse is here."

By this point, it had become obvious to everyone present that I was a policeman of some rank and in charge of the events that were unfolding. People were beginning to whisper.

I turned and faced the group, cleared my throat, and said, "Ladies and gentlemen, if I can have your attention. My name is Joel Franklin, and I'm a detective with the London Police Force. By chance, my wife and I were attending tonight's séance with our friend Celeste Bedgegood.

"By now, you are all aware of the tragic death of Mr. Chavin. After a brief discussion with the coroner, I believe that Mr. Chavin may not have died from natural causes."

There were some ohs and ahs from the crowd, some tears from Mr. Chavin's friends among the older generation, and many worried faces.

"With the help of the constables, I will need to get a brief statement from everyone present. I'm sorry to say that it may be a little while before you can go home. Please do not try to leave before we have given you permission. Mrs. Watkins has extended her hospitality to ensure that your wait will be as comfortable as possible. Coffee and other refreshments will be available, and a doctor should be arriving shortly for anyone who is feeling unwell."

I went over to where Georgie and Celeste Bedgegood were sitting on the sofa and said, "I'm going to be here for quite a while. I can vouch for you two and Paul, so you can all leave."

Georgie and Celeste looked at each other and said, "We're not sure we want to leave."

"I haven't had this much excitement in forty years," said Celeste. "Between the unfortunate death of Mr. Chavin and the fireworks at the séance, there are a lot of mysteries to be explained."

Georgie nodded vigorously in agreement.

"And I'm afraid they won't be explained until I get on with my investigation," I said.

"He's getting serious," said Georgie, pouting. "There's no arguing with him when he gets that look on his face. I guess we'll have to go, Celeste."

"Well, I won't insist," said Celeste. "Never get between a man and his work, as my mother always told me. After Paul drops me off at Central Ave., he can take you home, Georgie."

I motioned for Paul to join us while Georgie helped Celeste to her feet. I cleared them with the constables, and soon they were on their way out the door.

Three down, thirty-two to go.

Cst. Carmichael and I began taking information, while Cst. Johnson kept lookout, making sure that nobody wandered off.

We interviewed those on the periphery of the investigation first. The five remaining chauffeurs, the gardener, and the handyman, none of whom had been present in the drawing room, were quickly dispatched after taking down their names, addresses, phone numbers, and any pertinent observations they may have had. The housekeeper and two maids were never in contact with Mr. Chavin and also summarily dismissed. The nurse had the medical expertise to apply the poison, but she had been on the other side of the mansion and had no personal connection to Mr. Chavin, so she was returned to her duties as well. The cook and her assistants bore closer inspection, but as none of the other guests had been poisoned, and Robinson believed the agent to be cyanide and not food poisoning, and the cook and her assistants had no personal connection to Mr. Chavin, they were released after a brief interview.

Eighteen down, seventeen to go. Over halfway. Now we were approaching the more directly relevant witnesses. The butler and his two aides were present in the drawing room and in a position to administer poison, but they were all in good standing and had long been employed by Mrs. Watkins. Additionally, they had no obvious motivation for poisoning Mr. Chavin, so there was no reason to suspect them. None of them had seen anything unusual. Barbara Watkins's son, his wife, and their children had nothing to add beyond what I'd already gathered from them.

Dr. Smith had arrived during our earlier interviews, and he had checked on all the older people. He reported that they all seemed to be calm now, and that there were no imminent health concerns.

"The only person that seems to be in medical distress is that tall, sophisticated-looking man with the pince-nez," Dr. Smith said. "His blood pressure is quite high. I suspect it's due to the fact that he hasn't received special treatment by being placed at the front of the interview line."

I thanked the doctor, and he volunteered to stay until the end of the interviews, just in case. He helped himself to a drink, cordially provided by one of the cook's assistants.

Having eliminated twenty-six people, the crowd in the drawing room now seemed much more manageable. So far, nothing untoward had surfaced. But even with two people conducting interviews, over two hours had passed. We took a short break, and coffee and Violet Murphy's June muffins were served.

There were only nine people remaining. Those left to be interviewed included Dr. Plimpton, who was in a state of outrage; his two assistants, Simon and Simone, who looked nervous and weary; the five older women; and one husband, Mr. Brightman.

As it was growing late, and I was no longer concerned about someone slipping away, I enlisted Cst. Johnson to interview three of the séance regulars, Marian McKelvie, Martha Brightman, and Alice Mulder. I told him to get the same information we'd obtained from the staff and other guests.

Then I turned to Cst. Carmichael and said, "I need you to help me interview the last six people. I'll conduct the interview, while you record the answers. It will take a little more time, but in the event something significant arises in the interview, or there is a subsequent disagreement, I'll have you as a witness.

"We'll conduct these six interviews privately," I said. "Mrs. Watkins said I can use her office. It's right next to the drawing room. Let's go to her office for a moment and arrange the furniture to make it conducive for interviews."

As we started to walk towards the office, Dr. Plimpton suddenly appeared in front of me and sputtered, "Where are you going, Detective? This is no time for you to take a break. I have to leave early tomorrow morning—in a few hours—I've got another important engagement back in the United States."

"Calm down, please, Dr. Plimpton," I said. "I wasn't taking a break; we're using Mrs. Watkins's office for the remainder of our interviews. Please take a seat; the sooner we get on with it, the sooner you'll be able to leave. We'll call you in a couple of minutes."

Dr. Plimpton turned abruptly, muttering under his breath. Carmichael gave me a rueful smile and we continued on to the office.

Once we had the office ready for use, I said to Carmichael, "Go and get Dr. Plimpton. We might as well get this over with."

Cst. Carmichael appeared within the minute along with Dr. Plimpton. The doctor appeared to be marginally mollified by having been taken first from among those left to be interviewed.

"Please take a seat, Doctor," I said.

The doctor seated himself, fussing imperiously with his collars and pince-nez.

"I can see I was mistaken about you, Mr. Franklin," he muttered. "You are not a fellow seeker after the higher truths, but a common skeptic."

"That's Det. Franklin," I said curtly.

I started the interview with routine questions, taking his name, telephone number, address, occupation, and reason for being at Mrs. Barbara Watkins's residence this evening. Cst. Carmichael wrote everything down.

"You know all of that, why are you wasting my time?" snapped Dr. Plimpton.

"In my line of work, it's hardly wasted time," I said. "It's standard procedure, and it's necessary. I—and the courts—rely on the information that you give at the start of an interview recorded in front of a witness."

Dr. Plimpton visibly flinched when I used the word 'courts.' I finally had his full attention.

"You will find some of my questions tedious," I said. "I ask that you cooperate and give concise answers, that way the interview will be over sooner."

Dr. Plimpton slumped in his chair, deflated, and said, "Fine."

"Is this the first séance you've conducted at Barbara Watkins's residence?" I asked.

"Yes. I must confess," he said, perking up a little, "the elaborate preparations she made ahead of time for the séance were excellent. I was delighted to be able to hold a séance here."

Now that he'd consigned himself to being interviewed, he seemed eager to talk.

"Have you conducted séances for other people in London?"

"Yes, there's a whole little group of them," he said proudly.

"Tell me about the previous séances you've conducted for this group of people in London."

Prior to the séance tonight, Dr. Plimpton informed us, he had conducted séances at the residences of the Chavins and Brightmans, and at the home of Celeste Bedgegood. Dr. Plimpton then went on at some length about how fortunate the city of London was to have been the site of four of his best séances.

Cst. Carmichael looked at the clock. I asked Dr. Plimpton, "How well did you know Edward Chavin?"

"I'd been introduced to him," said the doctor. "He was an excellent host while I was at their home, but the husbands have never been part of the séance group. They're materialists, not spiritualists. So I never had an extended conversation with him. I really don't know anything about him."

"Do you know of any reason why someone might want Mr. Chavin dead?" I asked.

"No, as I told you before, I know nothing about him," said Dr. Plimpton brusquely.

"Dr. Plimpton, why did you try to flee after the death of Mr. Chavin?"

This question floored the doctor.

"Wh-wh-what? Flee? What do you mean?" he stammered.

"I mean, why did you abruptly leave Mrs. Watkins's when it was revealed that Mr. Chavin was dead?"

For almost a full minute, the doctor seemed unable to reply. His face went through such a diversity of expressions that whether he was using the time to come up with a convincing alibi or he was genuinely perplexed by the question was impossible to determine.

"Yes, I can see..." he said finally. "I see now how suspicious that must have looked in retrospect, but believe me, Detective, at the time I had no idea it was about to turn into a criminal investigation. I simply thought ... well, I was very alarmed by the whole thing, not only the death of Mr. Chavin, but the phenomena in the séance chamber. I wasn't thinking clearly, I just knew that I wanted to get as far away from here as possible.

"I was also concerned about the repercussions the incident might have on my reputation. If people began to think my events were dangerous ... I thought if ... well, I don't know what I was thinking. I thought if I got away fast enough, I suppose, that maybe I could convince people that the death happened after the séance not during. I'm not proud of what I did, and I see now how futile it was now, but, as I said, I wasn't thinking clearly."

This seemed to tally with what Carmichael had told me earlier, but whether it was the truth or a lie only time would tell. I looked over at the constable and he gave me a slight nod to indicate that he'd taken the statement down and I could continue.

I turned to my second area of inquiry. "Tell me what happened at the end of this evening's séance."

Dr. Plimpton turned pale and said, "You were there in the octagon, Detective, you know what happened. You saw the lights and heard the growling."

"As a spiritualist, do you have any opinions on those phenomena?" I asked.

"It's never happened before," he said. "We communicate exclusively through the board." He paused and, with a serious expression, added, "Do you think those strange events had anything to do with Mr. Chavin's death?"

I declined to answer his question and instead asked, "Were you responsible for any of those special effects? The lights and the growling, as you put it."

Dr. Plimpton rose angrily to his feet and shouted, "Absolutely not! That is an outrageous accusation! I won't stay and listen to insults!"

Cst. Carmichael stood.

"It's not an insult, Doctor, it's a question," I said loudly and firmly. "And unless you want my constable to escort you back to the drawing room, where you will remain until all of the other interviews have been completed and you've had time to cool off, you will sit down so that we can continue with the remainder of this interview."

Dr. Plimpton, visibly shaking, face flushed with rage, glared at me for a moment, and then reluctantly resumed his seat.

Cst. Carmichael sat back down.

"Answer my question, please," I said.

"I am not a charlatan, Detective," he said haughtily. "I am a world-renowned Doctor of Thaumaturgy. I do not use special effects. I do not need to. I am a conduit between those who wish to speak to the spirits, and to the spirits who wish to communicate with the living."

Cst. Carmichael snorted involuntarily, though he tried to cover it up by pretending to clear his throat. This resulted in a scathing look from the doctor.

"So, you've never had noises or lights at any of your previous séances?" I asked the doctor.

"I've never experienced it before," Dr. Plimpton said in an unsteady voice. "I was just as surprised as you were. It was quite unnerving. I began to wonder if, somehow, we had conjured up an evil spirit. But that doesn't make sense. The octagon, the pastel-coloured panels, the white candles lit by the purple candle, all those things are positive in nature, designed to produce well-being. It should have protected us."

"Well, it does happen," I said a little louder than I intended to. "I've experienced it before."

Dr. Plimpton was startled. He looked at me fearfully and backed away a bit from the interview table.

"Don't be alarmed, Dr. Plimpton. I'm not an invoker of 'evil spirits.' I'm not a medium for ectoplasm with hellish intent. I'm just a person who's had more than their share of experience with the dead."

I wasn't too proud to admit to myself that I felt some delight on seeing the reaction I'd caused in him. I had to remind myself not to be mean despite my dislike of the pompous fraud.

"You said I was nothing but a common skeptic, but you're wrong, Doctor," I continued. "This is not the first time I've encountered these phenomena."

Now the doctor was even more alarmed. I could tell he was almost afraid to ask when he said, "W-where ... have you seen these ... phenomena?"

I could tell Cst. Carmichael was getting nervous too. "Where was that, sir?" he asked.

"Do you remember crazy Willie Porter the bank robber?" I said.

"Oh yes, I remember him," said Carmichael. "The haunted house at 62 Grover Lane in Louisburg, where Willie Porter grew up. The house with all the bodies in the basement."

Dr. Plimpton's eyes grew wide, appearing almost twice as large behind his pince-nez.

I stared into those terrified eyes and said, "You can take my word for it, Doctor, I was there. The noises and lights there were far worse than anything that happened here tonight."

Dr. Plimpton remained glued to his chair, which he'd pushed as far back from the desk as he could in the confined room. He seemed to be afraid of me, as if he thought I might be contagious.

I'd had my fun, but I didn't think I'd get much more out of the interview with Dr. Plimpton at this time. I wasn't sure whether the theft at Celeste Bedgegood's home had anything to do with this evening's events, and I didn't want to ask him any questions about the séance at Mrs. Bedgegood's until I had more evidence. The death of Mr. Chavin had made my case significantly more complicated. My primary concern now was that if Dr. Plimpton returned to Michigan immediately, it could be difficult for me to question him again.

"Do you have any more séances scheduled in London in the next couple of weeks? I asked in a calmer tone.

"I have a séance scheduled for Marian McKelvie next Wednesday evening ... and the Brightman's the following Wednesday evening," Dr. Plimpton stammered. "But I'm not certain ... because of what happened this evening ... whether to continue with the séances or not."

"I'm quite certain you won't have the same experience again," I said. "As you said, it's never happened to you before. I believe this was a singular event. You let me know what you decide, and if you would like me to attend the next séance, please let me know."

"I will let you know within the next couple of days," he responded with some actual enthusiasm. I wasn't sure if he'd welcome my presence after the events of this evening, but I could tell he was relieved and pleased that I had volunteered to attend the next séance. Perhaps he believed my greater experience in this area would provide him with some protection. The world-renowned Doctor of Thaumaturgy had been shaken to the core by tonight's events. His confidence and arrogance had both taken a severe blow.

Now that I felt confident he would be in London for the next two weeks, I decided to terminate his interview.

"That will be all, Doctor. Thank you for your cooperation."

Cst. Carmichael and I proceeded to interview first Simon and then Simone. They appeared to be even more traumatized by the noises and lights in the inner séance sanctum than Dr. Plimpton had been. They too had never experienced anything like it before. When they heard about my experience in Willy Porter's house, and that I had experienced those phenomena before, they were even more concerned about doing another séance.

No new information came from their interviews. They corroborated Dr. Plimpton's story about trying to escape the bad publicity. They had heard the doctor mention it repeatedly, and, like him, had had no idea that Mr. Chavin's death had turned the drawing room into a crime scene. When Dr. Plimpton had rushed them out the door, they'd simply gone along with him. He was their employer, after all. Though they had been introduced to Mr. Chavin, they knew nothing about him, and had no reason to poison him. Surmising that Simon and Simone would be in London for the next two weeks with Dr. Plimpton if I required them for further questioning, I let them go.

Though Mrs. Watkins's had done her best to console Irma, Mrs. Chavin was still extremely upset. Her husband's body had been removed to the morgue from Barbara Watkins's house while we were interviewing Dr. Plimpton. Considering the shock, and her advanced age, she was physically and morally exhausted, so after getting her name, address, and phone number, I thought it best to postpone any further interview with her until the next day at the earliest.

We interviewed Mrs. Watkins next. Though the murder had taken place in her home, and she had ample opportunity—and possibly motive—she'd been in the séance chamber with us when Mr. Chavin died, and she could tell us nothing that we didn't already know. She claimed to have no idea why anyone would want Mr. Chavin dead.

One stray detail from the séance did linger in my mind which I hoped she could clear up.

"During the séance," I started, "Alice Mulder tried to make contact with Bernice—"

"Oh yes, that's her daughter," said Barbara, intuiting my question. "Bernice disappeared twenty-four years ago while the family was camping up north. Alice attends every séance and asks for Bernice every time. She always gets an answer, either through the board or through knocking. It was Alice who got us into these séances. She was the one who found Dr. Plimpton and introduced him to our circle."

"Thank you, Barbara. That will be all," I said.

That left one person to be interviewed, Arthur Brightman. He was the last person to speak to Edward Chavin before he died.

After getting Mr. Brightman's personal information, I asked him, "How well did you know Edward Chavin?"

"I really didn't know him that well. I had never met the man until our wives got caught up in these séances. I know he's very wealthy, but I don't know where his money came from."

"You were talking to him tonight. What did you talk about?"

"Well, to be honest, the first thing we talked about was you."

"Why was that?"

"You and your wife appeared at this séance out of the blue and were announced as friends of Celeste Bedgegood. I didn't pay much attention to it, but Edward was suspicious and wondered why you were here. And then when he pointed out that you hadn't attended Celeste's séance, I began to wonder myself. It was very unusual to suddenly have two new séance members, especially two complete strangers."

"We're friends of Celeste's," I said. "My wife was quite interested in attending a séance, and I was quite interested in seeing the famous Dr. Plimpton in action.

"What other things did you talk about tonight?"

"We were both very impressed by the octagonal room that Barbara Watkins had prepared for the séance," said Mr. Brightman. "We talked quite a bit about the design and workmanship. Edward asked me if Martha and I had any special plans for our séance."

"Are you still planning to go ahead with it?" I asked.

"I am, but Martha is worried that what happened in the octagon will happen to us. I wasn't there, so I didn't get the full effect, but I saw the glow and I heard the growling. I'm a skeptical fellow, so I suspect it was all special effects. I think our Doctor of Thaumaturgy is trying to liven things up a little." Mr. Brightman chuckled.

"In general, how would you describe Edward's mood?" I asked him.

"I've only talked to him briefly at a couple of the other séances, but he always seemed to be in good spirits. Tonight, he seemed agitated."

"Did he talk to anybody else tonight in the drawing room while you were waiting for the séance to end?"

"No, he didn't. Even when the maid came around with the hors d'oeuvres and some glasses of champagne, he waved his hand sort of rudely and said that he didn't want any, instead of saying the customary 'No, thank you.'

"Mind you, he had his own whisky flask in his jacket pocket. He took a couple of drinks from it surreptitiously, and I pretended I didn't see what he was doing. He obviously had no intention of offering me any."

Here, in the last interview of the evening, after many long hours and not anticipating any new revelations, all of a sudden, in an off-hand comment, there was a mention of something that could be vital to the investigation. I had to find out about the contents of that whisky flask. Perhaps Arthur Brightman was fortunate he hadn't been offered a drink.

I excused myself and said I would return in a couple of minutes. I walked down the short hall to the drawing room and saw that one of Mrs. Watkins's maids was tidying up the room. I asked her where the closest telephone was. I didn't want to use the one in the office with Mr. Brightman sitting there.

The maid escorted me to the main hall and pointed to the telephone on the small table. I called Victoria Hospital and asked if the coroner, Dick Robinson, could be fetched to the telephone.

When Dick came to the phone and recognized my voice, he said, "You've really messed up my Wednesday evening, Joel. I hope you understand how much I appreciate that. My wife had to go and visit her mother by herself."

I could all but see his smile coming through the telephone.

"Maybe someday you'll return the favour," I said. I was glad I'd sent Georgie home where she couldn't overhear our conversation.

"What can I help you with?" he asked.

"Quick question for you, Dick—"

Before I could say more, he replied, "Yes, I found the flask in his pocket, and yes, it's the source of the cyanide. The fingerprint man has the flask now and is examining it."

"Thanks, Dick."

I returned to Barbara Watkins's office to continue the interview with Arthur Brightman.

"This is a difficult question, Mr. Brightman, because it's always very disturbing to be present when someone dies. Did Edward Chavin try to say anything to you before his sudden death?"

"No, he just suddenly looked very unwell and then he fell to the floor."

"Thank you," I said.

I concluded the interview.

I was exhausted, but I knew my evening wasn't over. I expected a pretty intense grilling about this evening's events from Georgie when I got home.

Thursday, June 15th

It's a good thing that I trust Georgie not to say anything to her best friends, or the neighbours, or her family, because I tell her more than I should. It's just that I find her input very helpful. She's very intuitive and has a knack for seeing what's important without being distracted by peripheral or nonessential details.

This morning, Georgie was waddling around the kitchen, getting the coffee ready and making toast. We had a long talk last night when I got home, and Georgie was still mulling things over this morning. During breakfast, she said to me, "I think the theft of the British biscuit box and its contents from Celeste Bedgegood's home, the death of Edward Chavin, and the pyrotechnical display at Barbara Watkins's séance are all connected. I just can't imagine how."

"The entire combination is an enigma to me," I confessed. "But my experience as a detective has taught me that the world is really like one big puzzle: if I work away at what seem to be separate pieces—separate facts—other pieces appear, and eventually the pieces—the facts—fit together. Of course, sometimes those other pieces *don't* appear; then, instead of one puzzle, I'm looking at two or more individual puzzles. Or, in this case, crimes. You always have to keep an open mind. But, in any event, you have to keep turning over new pieces to find more information. Sooner or later, no matter how confusing it seems at first, the puzzle, or puzzles, will solve itself, or themselves."

Georgie smiled at me and said, "That's a heavy bit of thinking from someone who can't usually manage much more than 'please pass the jam' in the morning. You must've been lying awake part of the night preparing that philosophical comment."

I smiled back at her and said, "I'm more than just a pretty face."

Georgie smiled and made no comment. Clearly, she was taking pity on me. She put a plate of toast down in front of me and said, "I imagine the thing that's in the forefront of your mind this morning is, 'Why did an essence appear at the séance?'"

"That's a loose thread I intend to pull at," I said, picking up my knife. "I'm just not sure how to approach it yet. Please pass the jam."

I had no sooner arrived at the detective section at the police station than Inspector O'Neill approached my desk and, with another sympathetic smile, said, "You have my condolences in advance, Joel. Chief Bedgegood wants to see you ... *now*."

I got up from my desk with more than a little trepidation.

When the chief interviewed me last Friday about my visit with his aunt Celeste, he had ended up in an almost apoplectic state. I had left that meeting in a condition of near shellshock. I understood the chief's vexation wasn't personal, but I certainly didn't enjoy being berated when I had done nothing to deserve it.

"Ah, Joel," the chief said when I entered his office, "thank you for coming by so soon. I need to know what happened last night at Barbara Watkins's mansion. All of a sudden, this is a huge story for the *London Free Press*."

With the words 'London Free Press,' on which he had placed unusual emphasis, he became a little pinker.

"Sir, I ... I have no idea how anybody found out about last night's events," I stammered. "There was no one there from the newspaper covering the séance. We didn't allow anyone into the house during questioning."

"Well, someone has talked," snapped the chief. "I had a call this morning from the editor-in-chief of the paper asking for an appointment at ten o'clock this morning with his top reporter. He wants to interview me, or someone connected to the case, about the murder and ... how did he describe it? ... 'the frightening display of lights and noises' at the séance. Now, what can you tell me?"

"First, Chief, so far as I can tell, there is no connection between the suspicious death of Edward Chavin and the events in the inner séance room. It's far too early in the investigation for us to make any comment."

"That's precisely the approach I was going to take," said the chief. "But I don't like being blindsided, Detective. So, off the record, tell me what in the blazes went on."

I gave the chief a detailed account of what I had seen and heard, and of what I had been able to determine, and answered his questions as accurately as I could. When I finished, the chief, still a mild pink colour, said to me, "I talked to the coroner earlier this morning. Edward Chavin was definitely poisoned. Someone added cyanide to whatever he was drinking from his pocket flask. As of this moment, we're considering it a homicide.

"I want you to continue with the case. But I'm also bothered by what happened in the séance room. As unusual as it seems, maybe there is a connection between the two events. I think you told me that when you were in the séance chamber, my aunt asked, 'Who's the thief?' just before the person outside in the drawing room started shouting, 'He's dead! He's dead!' about Edward Chavin. That's a little peculiar, don't you think? It's a strange coincidence, and I don't like coincidences."

The chief cast a glance at me and coloured a little.

"I certainly don't believe in séances or spirits," he added hastily, "but I do recall what happened at the house in Louisburg. I suppose, during the course of our investigation of Mr. Chavin's death, we can attempt to see what other unusual circumstances may have prompted the display in the séance chamber. I trust you will use your best investigative techniques, Joel."

"I'll do my best, sir," I said.

"By the way, you probably noticed I didn't shout at you once today," he said, beaming. A debatable point, but I wasn't about to argue over it. "My self-control isn't much better, but I am taking my blood pressure medication regularly. I'll need it to get through this bloody interview."

I had talked to Barbara Watkins briefly before I'd left her residence last night and explained to her that, because of the suspicious death of Edward Chavin, nothing in the drawing room, including the octagonal chamber, could be touched until we had completed a thorough examination of the crime scene. I'd told her that I would have two policemen at her home at nine o'clock Friday morning to begin the examination, and said I hoped to be there by ten.

When I arrived at Barbara Watkins's mansion, she answered the door herself. She appeared to be distracted, but she was very cordial and said, "I'm very pleased to see you, Det. Franklin. That was a terrible situation last night, and we were fortunate to have you present."

"Thank you," I replied. "Our examination of crime scenes can be very intrusive. We appreciate your cooperation. I'd better go and see how my constables are getting along."

Csts. Henderson and Bartlett had been sent to the forensic lab in Toronto for training. The medicolegal laboratory had been established there in 1932 by the deputy attorney general of Ontario and trained people from all over Canada. The two constables were far from expert, but they had a much better idea of what to look for than I did.

When I arrived in the drawing room, they were removing one of the panels from the octagonal base. There were only two panels left to remove.

"Have you found anything?" I asked.

"No, there don't appear to be any electrical connections of any kind in the panels," said Cst. Henderson. "Nothing to explain the fireworks. Bartlett and I are sure that it's what it appears to be, but we're taking it apart so we can see what's underneath the base. We're also wondering what's beneath this floor."

I didn't think the construction of the octagonal séance room had anything to do with the murder, but in an investigation it's worth checking every nook and cranny. I valued their enthusiasm and diligence.

"I'll talk to Mrs. Watkins and see if there's a room beneath the drawing room," I told them.

I found Mrs. Watkins perched nervously on a chair in the drawing room, gazing out the window. When I asked to see the cellar below the drawing room, she hesitated and then said, almost to herself, "I guess it's okay to let you into that room."

"I'd appreciate that," I said, following her out of the drawing room. "We like to be thorough in our investigations."

"Rodney," she said, calling to a young man in a starched shirt and waistcoat sitting in the hallway. "Would you show the detective downstairs to the office?" Mrs. Watkins turned to me with a frown and said, "Please don't disturb anything in the room. That room is my husband's private domain. Roger meets with a small group of friends there, and they conduct business of some kind. It's basically out of bounds to the rest of us."

I thanked Mrs. Watkins and returned to the drawing room, where Csts. Henderson and Bartlett were removing the last panel.

"When you're done here," I said, "the butler's aide, Rodney, will take us down to that cellar area below the drawing room."

Ten minutes later, the constables were satisfied, and Rodney led us to the main hall. He opened a large door and led us down a set of well-lit steps to the cellar below. The height of the cellar beneath the floor joists was over eight feet. It was higher than any cellar I'd ever been in before. A central hallway, with doors opening off on each side, ran the length of the cellar, mimicking the floor plan above. The hall, like the stairs, was well lit.

Rodney led us down the hallway. When we came to the second door on the left, he opened it and turned on a light. As we came through the door, we found ourselves in a large room. There was a beautiful regulation-size snooker table, approximately twelve feet long and six feet wide, ready for use, and we were sorely tempted by it, but duty called. About six feet away from the edge of the table, a makeshift wall consisting of numbered crates ran from the interior wall to within about four feet of the outside wall of the house. The crate wall was irregular in height, but in most places it reached to within a foot of the ceiling. When we went around the end of the wall through this opening into the other part of the room, we entered what appeared to be a meeting room. This part of the room contained a sturdy table about four feet long and six feet wide with five leather chairs around it. There were also four filing cabinets. There was nothing on the table.

"What's in the crates?" I asked Rodney.

"Mr. Watkins's collection of artifacts," he said. "They're from all over the world. He did a lot of traveling when he was younger. The contents are all recorded by crate number in a big book. Of course, he has the best ones on display upstairs. Only ... I don't think I can let you look in the crates, sir. Not without Mr. Watkins's permission."

"That's okay, Rodney, I won't need to look in them today," I said. "You can return your duties. I'll let you know when we're finished down here."

"Yes sir," he said. "Mrs. Watkins told me to be available in the drawing room in case there's anything else you need this morning." Before he left, he added nervously, "Please don't disturb things, if possible. I'm the only staff member allowed into this area. Mr. Watkins and his friends have highly confidential business documents stored here."

After Rodney departed, I sat down at the table and took out my pad. I looked over my notes and jotted down a couple more things. I would have to interview Rodney later; he might have some information that would be helpful.

Csts. Henderson and Bartlett spent some time with their necks craned, examining the floorboards of the room above. They tapped the boards with their fingers and scratched their chins. They did this office space first, then proceeded to the area where the pool table was. It took them about thirty minutes to satisfy themselves that nothing had been done in the cellar room to access the séance chamber above. When they were finished, I sent them back to the upper drawing room.

I was now in the private meeting room by myself. I strongly suspected there was an essence, if not in this room, then somewhere nearby. The display the other night indicated that either the essence was very disturbed and powerful, or there was more than one of them. I had no idea who it might be, though, and as a result there was very little likelihood of making contact. I had nothing with which to construct an emotional bridge.

One possible connection was the séance. I was certain the essence had been aroused by the séance enough to respond dramatically when Celeste Bedgegood had asked, "Who's the thief?"

Calming myself, I shut my eyes and concentrated on the séance, visualizing the flickering candles and Celeste Bedgegood asking her dramatic question. As I focused on this scene, I also sent the message, "I can communicate with you if you wish. My name is Joel Franklin. I'm a detective, and I have the ability to send and receive messages with people who have passed beyond. Please let me know you're here."

I waited but received no response. I opened my eyes and tapped my notebook impatiently. I couldn't spend too long here, or Rodney would be wondering what was going on.

I shut my eyes and sent another message. "I know you were treated unfairly. I'll do my best to help you. Please let me know if you're here."

Suddenly, I felt a chill, and I received an alarming message: "*The tiger!*"

It was a shriek of terror in my mind.

I almost lost the connection, but I calmed myself and sent: "What tiger?"

There was a moment of stillness, then, in a much calmer tone, I heard, "I was murdered in my own cellar."

Just then there was a knock on the door. I heard Rodney say, "There's a phone call for you, sir."

I went to the door and followed Rodney up the stairs to the telephone.

The voice of the other end of the line said, "Good morning, it's Dick Robinson. Sorry to drag you up from the cellar, Joel. I hope I wasn't interrupting anything important. I just thought I'd let you know we did find another set of fingerprints on that flask that Edward Chavin had in his pocket. We haven't been able to match them with anything yet, but they could be very helpful if you have a suspect."

"Thanks for the information, Dick," I replied. "Please let me know if you find anything else significant."

I asked Rodney if he would find Mrs. Watkins and ask her if she had a few minutes to talk to me. He returned a couple minutes later with Mrs. Watkins.

"I would like to talk to you for a few minutes in your office, if you have some time," I said.

"Certainly, that's not a problem," she answered.

Once we were seated, she said, "From your manner, I think that what you want to talk to me about is serious."

"It's possible it could be," I answered. "I've noticed that your husband wasn't present for the séance, and I haven't seen him around today."

Mrs. Watkins hesitated. She appeared to be troubled by something.

"Well, Roger doesn't like séances; he thinks they're a waste of time. He calls them foolish drivel. But I am a little worried about him. If I didn't hear from him today, I thought I would ask you to help me locate him. I know Roger and his close friends had a meeting in their office Monday night, down in the room that you just visited. It's not unusual for them, following a meeting, to go out for a late meal and some drinks, and occasionally they go to the Mulder's cottage in Port Stanley for a game of poker. But if Roger doesn't come home, he always telephones me the next morning to let me know he's okay. He didn't phone me Tuesday morning, but I know he was very upset with all the special preparations I'd gone to for what he called 'a silly séance,' so I thought he was just being difficult."

"I think the best information you could give me, if I am to track him down," I said, "would be a list of the names of those close friends who usually meet together with him in that room in the cellar."

"That's easy," she said. "Monday night Roger would've been meeting with Arthur Brightman, Jordan Mulder, Ambrose—or, as he prefers, Butch—McKelvie, and poor Edward Chavin."

I could see tears come to her eyes as she said Chavin's name. Out of curiosity, I asked, "Was Compton Bedgegood a member of the group before his death?"

"Yes, he was," she said, "he was a good man."

"I think I already have their addresses from last night. I'll have someone check with them, and we'll find out where Roger ended up."

I had my suspicions after the mysterious communication I'd received in Roger's office, but I didn't want to say anything to Barbara Watkins yet.

Friday, June 16th and Saturday, June 17th

I took Friday off. Our good friends Gwen Cummings and Dr. Alfred Khryscoff were getting married at St. James Westminster Anglican Church at two o'clock Saturday afternoon, and there were a lot of things to be done in preparation for the event.

Gwen and Alfred, who were both in their fifties and had never been married before, had been a little lost and overwhelmed by the process. Georgie had naturally and enthusiastically offered her assistance, but as the big day drew nigh, with my wife in an extremely pregnant state, I thought I should be handy just in case Junior came early. Besides, Alfred, whose nerves were more than a little frayed, needed the company.

It had been less than two months since Alfred's ordeal, when he'd been kidnapped and held hostage in a cottage up north by an old friend of his, Heinrich Smith. Heinrich had suffered a psychotic breakdown and, for a time, had posed a grave risk to the people closest to him. Though Alfred, a robust bear of a man, had recovered much of his former poise, I could tell that he was still in an emotionally fragile state. Alfred and I had worked on a number of cases together over the years, and I had learned much about the inner workings of abnormal psyches under his tutelage. I wouldn't have solved some of my most difficult cases without his help. While the women worked frantically to finalize the last-minute details of the wedding, Alfred and I stood on the porch, drinking whisky and smoking cigars, talking about the latest developments in psychiatry. We were shrewd enough judges of our own character to realize we would just be in the way.

It was to be a small wedding, fortunately, with only about thirty people attending. Neither Gwen nor Alfred came from large families, and neither had many living relatives. The Ladies' Auxiliary of the church was bearing a large part of the burden, but Gwen and Georgie's input was necessary if this was to be a great success. Everything had to look just right, not only at the church, but also at 78 Cedarwood Drive in London North, where Gwen lived with her aunt Agatha, and where the reception was to be held following the wedding supper at the church.

Gwen and her aunt Agatha had always been close. Since the death of Gwen's parents in a car accident more than ten years ago, Gwen had been spending more time with Agatha, and finally, last year, with Aunt Agatha in her mid eighties and needing some assistance, Gwen had sold her home in Chaseford and moved to London to live with her aunt on Cedarwood Drive. Gwen was one of the few people I'd met who shared my ability talk to essences, and her assistance had once saved my life and the life of a fellow constable, Peter Herman. Needless to say, seeing Gwen and Alfred happily married was important to me.

By eight o'clock Friday evening, things were in good shape. The church had been decorated, the rehearsal had gone smoothly, and the menu for the meal had been agreed on. We were all looking forward with excitement to the wedding at two o'clock the next day.

Georgie and I and Annie had our lunch earlier than usual on Saturday, so the three of us would have sufficient time to get dressed for the big wedding. The fancy outfits that Georgie and I wore to the séance on Wednesday evening had been cleaned, and, when we donned them, and when Annie had on her beautiful, pink flower girls' outfit, we looked like a royal couple with a princess. Though it had lightly rained that morning, the clouds were already parting to a gloriously blue sky, and the grass and leaves were sparkling like they'd been decorated with diamonds.

We were a little behind schedule, partly owing to the necessity for me to drive slowly, and for Georgie to take her time exiting the car and making her way into the church. At this penultimate moment, she wasn't about to take any chances.

We seated ourselves at a pew at the front and admired the work the Ladies' Auxiliary had done. The peonies decorating the church were especially gorgeous. Much as Gwen would have liked to have Georgie, as her matron of honour, standing beside her, with her due date so close, Gwen and Alfred thought it better to do without an official wedding party. Which meant that I got to sit too. Sitting beside us at the front pew, providing additional moral support, were an old college friend of Dr. Khryscoff's, and one of Gwen's cousins. Together, we made up the official unofficial wedding party.

The organist played beautifully. Soon everyone was in place. The wedding march began, Annie scattered petals with intense solemnity, and Gwen appeared at the door with an elderly uncle. Gwen and Alfred were not ostentatious people, and Gwen's gown was simple and tasteful. Alfred's nerves had recovered enough that he managed to assert his usual stately dignity, and Gwen did everything with such natural grace that you could hardly tell she was frazzled. She walked down the aisle without stumbling and Father Corrigan began the service with his resonant, musical Irish accent. There were tears in many eyes.

It was a lovely ceremony and would have been perfect had not a minor glitch occurred when Annie, the flower girl, blurted out, "I do!" in response to Father Corrigan's question to the bride. This caused a lot of laughter and a temporary interruption of the service. But not-quite-three-year-old flower girls are easily forgiven.

Monday, June 19th

Monday morning, I was back to a world that was very different from the beautiful celebration I had been a part of on the weekend. People were bustling about the station, phones were ringing, typewriters were clacking, lawbreakers were protesting their innocence. There was even a large dog in the station, barking loudly as its owner tried to restrain him.

I had spent quite a bit of time on Sunday recovering from the reception and thinking about the bizarre ending to the séance at Barbara Watkins's place last Wednesday night. That and my encounter the next morning with the essence that I believed to be her murdered husband, Roger Watkins. Much as I tried to fit the pieces together, I couldn't. The essence who spoke to me claimed to have been murdered in his own cellar, and yet there had been no body nor any sign of a struggle. Surely the servants would have stumbled across Roger Watkins's body by now. What we did have was the body of another man who'd died of cyanide poisoning in the drawing room directly above. Had the pyrotechnics been related to Roger's murder or Edward's? Or had they not been related at all? Had Roger Watkins been murdered during the séance at the exact same moment that Edward Chavin had died? This last idea was too incredible a coincidence to be believable, but that didn't make it impossible. And how did the murders fit in with the stolen items?

Last Thursday afternoon, I had told Cst. Carmichael I wanted him to contact Arthur Brightman, Jordan Mulder, and Ambrose McKelvie on Friday to see if they knew where Roger

Watkins might be. I warned him that Mr. McKelvie would probably be going by the name Butch instead of Ambrose. Shortly after I arrived at my desk in the detective section, Cst. Carmichael appeared with a report.

"So, what did you find out from Roger Watkins's friends?" I asked over the barking of the dog.

"They all reported that Roger Watkins was still in his office when they left his house Monday night," said Carmichael. "They said they'd held their regular meeting, that there were no major disagreements, and that Roger seemed to be in fine spirits. Then they all went their separate ways. There were no inconsistencies between their reports."

"Did you sense that anyone was hiding anything?" I asked.

"Not really, sir, but all these men are wealthy businessman, and no doubt skilled at concealing their feelings when it's necessary."

"You sound cynical, Constable," I said.

The constable gave me a sour smile. "Sorry, sir, but I have an uncle who fits into that category, and I don't particularly care for him because of the way he treats others. Let's just say I wouldn't be surprised if they weren't telling the truth."

I was inclined to agree with the constable, but I kept that thought to myself.

I drove over to Talbot Street North, parked my car, and knocked on the front door. The butler, Jason, answered the door.

"It's good to see you again, Det. Franklin," he said.

I wasn't sure why it was a good thing to see a homicide investigator, but I guessed it was Jason's standard greeting to those he recognized.

"Thank you," I said. "Is Mrs. Watkins in? If she's here, I'd like to speak to her."

Barbara Watkins appeared a couple of minutes later and invited me to her office. Once we were seated, she said, her voice tremulous, "Is there any news of my husband's whereabouts?"

"I had one of my men interview all of your husband's friends that attended the business meeting here last Monday night. They said Roger was fine when they left, and that, as far as they knew, he had no plans to go anywhere that evening."

Mrs. Watkins started to cry quietly. "We've had minor disagreements from time to time, but he has always kept me informed of where he is going or where he has ended up. There's never been longer than twenty-four hours when I haven't heard from him. This is so totally out of character for him that I am very worried."

"With your permission, I would like to do a thorough search of the cellar," I said. "I would also like to look in those filing cabinets in your husband's office as well."

"I have no problem with you examining the cellar, but I think I should get a legal opinion about you looking in the filing cabinets. They don't contain any business of mine; I believe they're records from a registered company whose members include my husband and Arthur Brightman, Jordan Mulder, and Butch McKelvie."

"That makes perfect sense," I said. "The office will have to satisfy me for now. Oh, before I forget, how many other ways are there in and out of the cellar?"

"There's a side door into the cellar, not far from the stairs that you've been using to get down there, and there's also a door at the far end of the cellar. It's like a hatchway that goes out into our rear yard."

"Thanks," I said, getting up. "I'm going to go down and examine the office now. I prefer not to be disturbed unless it's urgent."

I went to the main hall, opened the large door, and went down the well-lit steps. It didn't take me long to find the side door near the stairs that led outside. This door appeared to give easy access from outside to a workroom and a storeroom filled with the sort of things a handyman or groundskeeper might need. I turned on the lights. There was no sign of a body, no trace of blood, and no sign of a struggle. I opened the door leading outside and found myself at the bottom of a set of stone steps. The stairwell wasn't particularly wide and relatively steep. From the bottom, you could see over the top bricks into a side yard that was clearly visible from next door.

I went back inside and began checking the rooms that we'd ignored on our last visit. I didn't have time to do a thorough investigation, nor did I have a warrant, but I was looking specifically for a body, which shouldn't have been hard to find if it hadn't been carefully hidden. There was a wine cellar, a fruit cellar, a cold storage room, and a lumber room. There looked to be at least two hundred years of old furniture and family heirlooms in that room, but there was no sign of a body or of any recent disturbance. There was one locked room which I would have to get permission to inspect. Finally, I went into the office and turned on the light. It looked undisturbed since the last time I'd been there, though there was a distinctive chill in the air.

I left the office and went into the rear part of the cellar, which was largely unfinished. There were a number of large barrels and a large number of wooden packing crates stacked against one wall, along with some odds and ends. There was also a large furnace, a coal room, and a room for firewood. I found the hatchway at the far end of the cellar. It was double-doored, relatively broad, and there were only five steps. Using the butt of a shovel leaning against the wall to avoid getting fingerprints on the handle, I pushed up one of the doors and looked outside. The yard was enclosed by a high hedge on two sides leading down toward the river. I shut the door and checked the floor more carefully, using my flashlight. I found traces of a path of disturbance in the dust on the floor leading from the hatchway to the cellar office. It was solid and rectangular—a rug, perhaps; heavy because it held the weight of a body. The path wasn't noticeable unless you were looking for it.

I re-entered the office and sat at one of the chairs next to the table. I concentrated, focusing on Roger and Barbara. As essences were a product of strong emotion, it was easiest to reach them by appealing to those emotions, and few bonds created emotions as strong as the bond of matrimony.

I sent the message, "It's Joel Franklin, the detective. Barbara misses you, Roger. She's worried."

After a brief wait, a message formed in my mind. "I love her," sent Roger. "She is alone now."

"Can you tell me about your death?" I sent.

"The meeting was over. Everyone was gone, or I thought they had. I was just finishing the minutes and updating our books when I heard a noise behind me. I half turned and saw something flashing out of the corner of my eye. I reached with my right hand and grabbed something, some kind of fabric, and then I felt a terrible pain in my eyes. I struggled to get up, but something held me down. I couldn't see. I grappled with someone, and I sensed, somehow, that I knew them, but I couldn't tell who it was. And then I felt a sharp pain in my chest, and I thought, 'I've been stabbed.' I was stabbed and stabbed again. It was like the tiger was there again, biting me, killing me. I could feel myself getting weak. I knew I was dying. I was pulled out of the chair. I was being dragged somewhere."

The communication ended.

I waited for a moment, then I tried to reach Roger again. There was no response.

I went back up to the main floor and found Rodney waiting in the main hall.

"What's in that locked room downstairs?" I asked him.

"That's where Mr. Watkins keeps his most valuable possessions," he said. "I've only been in it a few times, but I don't like it much. Mrs. Watkins makes him keep his animals there."

"His animals?" I said, mystified.

"Yes. The stuffed ones. All the taxidermy. It's like a haunted zoo. There's a big Bengal tiger in there, from his last hunting trip in India. It gives me the creeps. It looks like it's watching you wherever you go. Mr. Watkins was a big game hunter when he was younger, back in the 1890s."

Heinrich Smith, the man who'd abducted Alfred, had been a hunter too, though of the domestic variety. What was it with rich people and hunting?

"Can you let me in?" I said, suddenly very intrigued. I remembered the growls I'd heard during the séance.

"I don't have the key," said Rodney. "Mr. Watkins keeps it on him. Even Mrs. Watkins can't get in. He lets me in when he wants it dusted but keeps the key with him."

"Thank you, Rodney. You've been a big help."

I found Barbara Watkins in her office and confirmed that she didn't have the key for Roger's room.

"He gave all of that up when he got bit by the tiger," she said. "That was the last animal he ever killed. It nearly cost him his life. He used to have the beastly thing on display in the drawing room. A 'conversation piece,' he called it. The servants have never liked it. There's a rumour that it walks around the house at night when everyone is asleep. Silly stuff.

"I always hated that thing. We had an argument over it once, Roger and I, and I told him he could either have the tiger or his wife in the drawing room, but not both. He finally moved it downstairs along with the rest of his trophies. The menagerie, I call it. He always keeps the door locked, as if he's afraid of it getting out. If it were up to me, I'd burn it."

I talked to her for a few more minutes, then I headed back to the police station.

When I arrived at the police station, I went straight to Chief Bedgegood's office.

"Do you have a minute, sir?" I asked him.

"I have five minutes," said the chief. "Come in and tell me what the problem is."

"Do you know Roger Watkins, sir?"

"Certainly, his wife is a friend of my aunt's, and he is a very prominent member of the London community."

"I spoke to Barbara Watkins this morning," I said. "Her husband's been missing since last Monday night. Mrs. Watkins is very concerned because this is not usual for him. I examined his cellar this morning, where his home office is, and I'm concerned that something bad has happened to him. I would like permission to authorize a search for him in the immediate neighbourhood of his home. I'd also like a warrant to access one room that was locked."

"You have my permission to search the neighbourhood, but keep it low key," said the chief. "I don't want the *London Free Press* sticking their nose into this yet. As for the warrant, I frankly don't see it happening. Mr. Watkins is an important man, and at this point we don't have a good reason to go picking through his private possessions. For all we know, he's gone fishing. I'd forget about that for now, Detective."

I left the chief's office and immediately hunted for Cst. Carmichael. I didn't have far to look. Carmichael wants to become a detective, so, whenever possible, he hangs out in the vicinity of the detective section.

When I spied him, I said, "Cst. Carmichael, I want you and Cst. Johnson to find two other constables to do some door-to-door searching on Talbot Street North. This search has the chief's approval, and it's to be done in a low-key manner. You don't need to search the interiors of the homes; it's the rear yards and the land behind the properties running down to the Thames River that need to be carefully looked at. Contact the owners and get permission to go on the property and then conduct your search. You'll be looking for either a body or body parts, or a shallow grave, most likely. Also, check along the riverbank. If you're asked what you're looking for, tell them that you're looking for, 'evidence of a crime that may have been committed.' I want you to start the search as soon as possible."

"Yes sir," said Cst. Carmichael, obviously excited to be involved in a homicide investigation.

After he jogged away, I checked my watch. It was now about a quarter after eleven. That left me with about forty-five minutes before lunch to take a look at the notes that Cst. Johnson had produced Wednesday night when he'd interviewed Marian McKelvie, Martha Brightman, and Alice Mulder.

I opened the folder and read. There wasn't much in the notes. The only thing that was different from what I expected was a brief notation at the end of Alice Mulder's interview. Cst. Johnson had written down 'BBBC?' I'd have to talk to Johnson when I saw him; if someone else is going to read your report, you can't use short forms. BBBC didn't mean anything to me, and maybe it wasn't important, but I wanted to know what the letters stood for.

It was about four o'clock when the call came in. When I picked up my telephone, I heard, "We've found a body." Cst. Carmichael was breathless. He must've run to the nearest house to make the call.

"Where are you?" I asked.

"We're on the riverbank behind a neighbour's house, the Jensens'. It's the second house down from Barbara Watkins's place."

"Don't touch a thing," I said. "I'll get Dick Robinson, as well as Csts. Henderson and Bartlett, to take a look at the crime scene."

I made a hasty call to the coroner and then rounded up our two new forensic 'experts.' The four of us were there in less than fifteen minutes. Cst. Carmichael was there to greet us.

"It's right this way," he said, leading us along the side of the house to the back and down a slope to the Thames. A second constable was waiting for us there, not far from a patch of cedar trees, standing over a patch of disturbed earth. A third constable was combing the grounds nearby.

"Where's Cst. Johnson?" I asked Carmichael.

"He's inside, talking to the Jensens," he said.

I nodded and we walked over to the crime scene. The remains had been placed in a very shallow grave about ten feet away from the edge of the river. It likely would've gone unnoticed for some time except a dog or some other animal had dug enough of the earth away to reveal part of an arm and a face. The body was half-wrapped in a rug.

"What happened to his face?" I said, suppressing the urge to turn away. There was a queasy feeling in the pit of my stomach. I'd seen corpses before, but the bubbled black crust clinging to the corpse's skull was unlike anything I'd ever come across.

Robinson bent over the body and did a quick examination, then he turned to me and said, "Joel, my preliminary assessment is that these are severe acid burns. Probably sulphuric. He's also suffered some significant stab wounds."

This case was getting worse and worse.

Tuesday, June 20th

The coroner, Dick Robinson, called me first thing in the morning with his summary report. Roger Watkins had been stabbed to death; the acid, which was sulphuric, had most likely been used to blind him.

"Where would a person get sulphuric acid?" I asked Dick.

"It's used in lots of things," said Dick. "Fertilizer, explosives, glue. Lots of factories use it. It's not hard to get if you know where to look."

"What about cyanide?"

"Rat poison would be the easiest way to get it."

I made a note of this, but it didn't seem immediately helpful. Unlike hemlock, the agent in the first case of poisoning I'd ever encountered, when I was a still a teenager living in Chaseford, neither of these special agents seemed to be difficult to get or require any particular expertise to use.

Dick said he hoped to have the body cleaned up and available for viewing by one o'clock this afternoon. I thanked him and hung up.

I left the station and called on Barbara Watkins at her home on Talbot Street North. I was greeted at the door by the butler, Jason, who said, "It's good to see you again, Det. Franklin."

I don't think he meant it. As austere as he normally was, today he seemed to be downcast.

"Mrs. Watkins isn't feeling her best today," he said. "If you'll take a seat, I'll go and speak to her."

Jason returned a couple minutes later and said, "Mrs. Watkins will see you in her office."

Jason escorted me to the office. Mrs. Watkins was seated at her desk, staring at the framed photograph she held in her hand. There were dark circles under her eyes, and the wrinkles on her face seemed especially deep. She invited me in and, once I'd entered, said, "Please close the door."

It seemed a struggle for her to look away from the photo. Finally, she looked up at me with tears in her eyes and asked, "Have you found the body?"

"I believe we've found Roger," I said gently.

She nodded as if to say she'd expected as much.

"If you're able to, we'd like you to come down to the morgue at one o'clock this afternoon to identify the body," I said. I steeled myself and added, "He suffered some damage to his face, but not so much that you won't be able to identify him."

I didn't enjoy making that statement, but it was necessary to prepare her for what she might see at the morgue.

Mrs. Watkins rubbed the tears from her face and stood up with a heavy sigh. She turned and faced the window, overlooking the grounds.

"I'll be okay. I knew in my heart he was dead," she said. "I just can't believe that someone murdered him. Roger wasn't perfect. No one knows that better than I do. He was an aggressive businessman, and he could often be disagreeable, but he was never the type to deliberately harm someone. He had a very stringent code of honour, in his own way. I have no idea why anyone would want to kill him."

I knew violence didn't discriminate, and took the guilty and innocent alike, but this was hardly the time for a philosophical discussion.

"We'll do our best to find the guilty party," I said reassuringly.

As I turned to leave, Mrs. Watkins said, "One other thing, Detective: I talked to my lawyer yesterday afternoon, and he informed me that you wouldn't have permission to look in the filing cabinets in Roger's office until your request had been approved by a majority of the members of the board. The company files are stored there."

I did my best not to betray my frustration. "Do you know the name of the company and the members of the board?"

"Yes, that information the lawyer was able to give me," she said, picking up a sheet of paper from the desk. She put on her reading glasses and read, "The company is called Group of Six Investments. It was incorporated in 1919. The six original members constituted the board of directors. The original members were my husband, Roger Watkins, Compton Bedgegood, Edward Chavin, Jordan Mulder, Arthur Brightman, and Ambrose McKelvie. Ambrose is Butch's legal name."

"So, with of the death of Compton Bedgegood a number of years ago, and the more recent tragedies, there may now only be three surviving members on the board," I said, thinking out loud. I'd have to get approval from two of them.

Barbara nodded and said, "I have no idea what the group was up to, but I do know they took their business seriously. I'm sure there was a significant amount of money or property involved."

"Why do you say that?" I asked.

"Just from things Roger said. He never said anything specific, but one time he told me that when the company had finished its mission in July this year, it could mean a lot of money for us."

When I arrived back at my desk at the police station, I decided I'd better jot down some notes and attempt to organize the information I had. What was I involved in? Was this just one complicated investigation, or was it two separate investigations?

Item one. It had started less than two weeks ago, when Chief Bedgegood asked me to investigate what he suspected was a fraud being perpetrated against his aunt Celeste.

Item two. After talking with his aunt, it turned out that it wasn't a fraud, but rather the theft of a valuable artifact, a British biscuit box that contained many important documents.

Item three. The timing of the theft from Celeste seemed to coincide with a séance that had been held at her home.

Consequently, in following up this lead, I had attended another séance during which a man had been murdered by poisoning. That was *item four*.

Item five. The investigation of that death had resulted in an encounter with the essence of another man who had been recently murdered. A murder which I believe had occurred in the cellar office at the home of the latest séance, directly under the place where the first man had died.

I looked over my notes. I was still as confused as when I'd started. This was becoming a very complicated situation indeed.

I leaned back in my chair. I noticed the report from Cst. Johnson that I had left on the corner of my desk. The notation at the bottom of his interview of Alice Mulder, BBBC, was as good a loose thread as any to pull next.

I called the telephone number that Cst. Johnson had included in the report. After several rings, the phone was answered, and I heard, "Good morning, this is Alice Mulder."

"Good morning, it's Det. Joel Franklin. I was hoping you'd have a few minutes you could spare for me this afternoon to help me clear up a few details about last Wednesday evening?"

"What time would you be dropping over?" Alice asked.

"Three o'clock, if that would work for you," I said.

"Do you need to talk to my husband, Jordan?" she asked. "He's away, supervising some work on our cottage at Port Stanley. He won't be home until sometime this evening."

"No, I don't need to see him today," I said.

"Then I will see you at three o'clock this afternoon, Detective. Goodbye."

Barbara Watkins stood beside me as Dick Robinson pulled back the sheet covering the face of the body we had discovered yesterday.

She gasped and seemed about to collapse. I grabbed her by the elbow, steadying her. She kept her head averted for a moment or two, then looked again. I looked too. The left side of the corpse's face had been charred black. The eye looked like it had been eaten away. The right side of the nose was also severely seared, and the right eye a milky white. The disfigurement was extreme.

An odd choking sound escaped Barbara, and she turned away from the body in an attempt to regain control of herself. After a minute, she seemed somewhat composed.

"I'm q-quite certain that's R-roger," she said finally in a shaky voice. "There will be scars on the front and back of his left shoulder."

Dick pulled the sheet down a little farther, exposing several puckered white scars from what was obviously a bite from a large animal. The more recent wounds from the knife were also partly exposed. According to Dick, the first two stab wounds had been well off the mark, indicating some kind of struggle; the third, and deepest, went straight through the heart. Dick lifted and turned the body slightly, revealing the corresponding bite marks on the back of the shoulder.

"These are clearly from an animal," he said. "But I haven't been able to determine what type yet."

"A tiger," said Mrs. Watkins, her voice cracking. "That's my husband, Roger." Mrs. Watkins burst into sobs.

I escorted Mrs. Watkins back out to the reception area where her chauffeur was waiting. She signed for the box of her husband's personal effects, which she had requested, and before she left, I said, "I will get to the bottom of this. I will find the person who murdered your husband."

Alice and Jordan Mulder lived on the edge of south London, on Commissioners Road. The city hadn't surrounded them yet, and they had a nice parcel of land. The house was a white, three-storey Plantation-style dwelling with a sprawling veranda, huge white columns, and a second-floor balcony. The grounds were nicely landscaped, with many fine flowerbeds, and there was a small white barn behind the house.

Alice was working in her flowerbeds when I arrived. She looked up, raising the rim of her sunhat so she could get a look at me as I pulled up the lane.

"Good afternoon, Detective," she said when I got out of the car. "Lovely weather, isn't it? The dahlias are eating this sun up!"

I hadn't interviewed Alice last Wednesday night after the séance. She had been in the inner séance chamber with me when the noises and lights had occurred, shortly after I had heard her ask about her daughter Bernice. Now, when I met her at her home, behaving so unlike Barbara Watkins, I had the impression that she was a down-to-earth person, which seemed at odds with her belief in séances. She may have been over seventy years old, but her actions didn't demonstrate any frailty due to age.

Alice led me across the veranda into her house. It wasn't quite as big as Barbara Watkins's residence, but everything betrayed exquisite—and expensive—taste. I followed Alice through the front hall into the kitchen, where tea and strawberry scones awaited us. There must have been servants somewhere about.

"I've tried my best to recover from that awful evening," she said, taking off her gardening gloves and sitting down. "What a nightmare. I feel so sorry for Irma. I hope you can get to the bottom of that murder."

"We're working on it," I said, seating myself across from her, "and although it may take some time, I'm confident we'll find the killer."

"You said you had some questions for me," said Alice, pouring tea into my cup.

"Yes," I said, taking out my notebook. "They shouldn't take long."

"Well, I'll do my best to answer them," said Alice. After we'd fixed our tea, she said, "What's your first question, Detective?"

What I really wanted to ask Alice was if she knew anything about the Group of Six Investments company that her husband was involved in. But I was afraid that she would be offended by the question. That was her husband's business, not hers, and she might feel that I had put her in the position of informing on her husband. So I passed on that question.

Instead, I said, "Wednesday evening you were interviewed by Cst. Johnson—"

"Yes, I remember him," she said, interrupting me. "A very nice young man. It turns out that I know one of his aunts, Amelia O'Brien. She's a fine woman. I could tell you some stories about the times the two of us had together when we were younger."

Her eyes twinkled at the recollection, and I knew I had to act fast. I tried to recapture the interview by saying, "Cst. Johnson does a fine job. He's a good policeman. He wrote me a couple of notes after his interview with you. On the bottom of the page of the interview, he jotted down 'BBBC.' I haven't had a chance to ask him about it. Do you recall what those letters meant?"

"Oh yes, his aunt Amelia collects things too, and we got talking about the different things that people collect, and antiques, and history."

I could sense she was about to run away into a discussion of antiques, history, and lord only knew what else, so I attempted to get the interview back on track by saying, "The two of you had me baffled. What does BBBC mean?"

"Oh, I'm sorry, that's right, you did ask about that, and you don't know what it means. I'm not surprised; you're a man, so you're not likely interested in women's collectibles. However, I suppose as a man you collect things too. What do you collect, Detective?"

"I mostly collect interesting facts," I said, once more attempting to regain control of the conversation. The scattered nature of Alice's conversation was becoming disorienting. "I'd love to know what BBBC means."

I waited in trepidation, not certain into which area the conversation would venture next. Third time's a charm.

"'B' for British, 'B' for biscuit, 'B' for box, and 'C' for club," she said, enumerating them on her fingertips.

With an impolitic hint of incredulousness, I said, "There's an actual club?"

For a moment I feared I may have insulted her, but apparently not, for with a smile she continued, "It's an important club in this city, Detective. We have one of the best BBB clubs in North America."

"My goodness," I said, more surprised than impressed. "You must be proud to be a member."

"I certainly am," she agreed, glowing. "I'm this year's president."

"Who are the other members of the club?" I asked, certain I already knew the answer.

"You are a very fortunate young man," she said. "I believe you've met all the members. One of them is your good friend Celeste Bedgegood. The others, aside from me, are Barbara Watkins, Martha Brightman, Marian McKelvie, and Irma Chavin."

"Are these antique British biscuit boxes valuable?" I asked.

"Yes, certainly. Many of them are very valuable, young man."

I had been called young man and detective a couple of times now, and I was wondering if she could remember my name.

"Amongst the six of us, I believe our collection would be worth well over $200,000," Alice said.

I was speechless. That did boggle my mind.

I tried to get my mind back on track. I was almost done, but she wasn't finished.

"Some terrible things have been happening to our collections," she said, pausing to scrutinize me to make certain I was paying attention. "Our best British biscuit boxes are disappearing."

I was suddenly quite interested again. I had a hunch, and I wanted it verified, so I asked, "Have all six of you lost British biscuit boxes?"

"No, and that's what's confounding," she said. "Marian McKelvie and Martha Brightman haven't lost any boxes. I didn't think Barbara Watkins had any missing either, but last weekend when I was talking to her, she told me that three of her most valuable British biscuit boxes had disappeared too."

I thought I now knew what was happening to the British biscuit boxes. And I thought I knew who was involved. Now I would have to set a trap.

I thanked Alice for the tea and scones, and for her help, and escaped to my car.

Wednesday, June 21st

"Can you believe there's another séance tonight, Georgie?" I said, adjusting my tie in the mirror.

"No, I can't believe it," said Georgie from the bed. "That tragedy at Barbara Watkins's was only a week ago. I'm not sure why the urgency to hold the next séance so soon."

"You and I aren't believers, Georgie, but I guess, for those who are, séances are extremely important."

"'Not believers' is a strange thing to hear from someone who speaks to ghosts on a regular occasion," said Georgie, propping herself up against a stack of pillows.

"Essences, dear. And I don't mean believers in ghosts; I mean believers in Plimpton. How's the tie?" I turned to face her.

"As straight as it ever is or ever shall be," said Georgie. "Come here and I'll fix it."

"Dr. Plimpton was booked several months ago to conduct the séances here in London," I said as Georgie wrangled with my tie. "The first four séances have been held, but he still has a booking at the McKelvie residence tonight, and his final booking at the Brightman's home on Wednesday, June 28th. Dr. Plimpton has to leave London by Friday, June 30th, because he has other séances booked in cities all across North America, and he won't be back in the London area again for at least a year."

"It sounds like you've memorized his itinerary," she said, tugging the tie. "So, you don't think he's too frightened to go ahead with the séance?" she asked with a devilish grin.

I couldn't help but smile.

"I'm convinced he's genuinely worried about it," I said, kissing her on the tip of her nose, "but because he's only encountered lights and noises this one time at Watkins's, I think he's overcome his fear. Although he's asked me to be present just in case." I took my jacket off the back of the chair and slipped it on. "Did you want to go to the séance with me tonight?"

"I'm going to pass," said Georgie, with a wince as she shifted her weight. "I'm not feeling that comfortable today, Joel. I wouldn't be surprised if Junior comes sometime very soon." She patted her belly and smiled.

After returning from Alice Mulder's home yesterday, I had dropped in to the station to see Chief Bedgegood for a minute. I'd told him what I suspected and had asked his permission to have a few extra constables on duty tonight around the McKelvie home.

"If you think your plan for this evening might result in my aunt Celeste getting her British biscuit box back, with all the papers it contained, I'm in favour of your request," he'd said. "I'll even request that Insp. Simpson have his trained squad on the grounds tonight."

"That would be very helpful, sir," I'd replied. "He has an excellent team. Please remind him I don't want anybody shot."

Chief Bedgegood had grinned, as if the thought didn't entirely displease him.

"After I've talked to him, Joel, I'll have him come and talk to you about the details of your plan."

This morning, half an hour after I arrived at the station, Insp. Simpson appeared at my desk.

"The chief said you need my help tonight at a séance. Is some evildoer being called back from the dead? If we arrest him, I don't know whether our cells will hold him, Joel. He might just slip through the walls." Insp. Simpson chuckled.

"No, this time we're after some very much living thieves," I told him. "I want you to deploy your men out of sight around the McKelvie estate. Do you know where that is?"

"Yes, it's on the edge of London North, just outside of town." The inspector thought for a moment. "It's a big house, fifty acres overlooking the city. I'm going to need all my men."

"That's the place," I said. "I'd like your men in place by half past five, if that's possible. Don't stop anybody from going onto the property, but please stop anybody that leaves the property. I want all bags, suitcases, parcels, and cars searched thoroughly unless they have a note signed by me."

"What are we looking for?"

"Valuable antiques," I said. "And biscuit boxes."

Insp. Simpson gave me a look. "Are the thieves stealing cookies?"

I had made arrangements to go to the séance with Celeste Bedgegood, and I showed up at her door in my tux. She was glad I was going, but she was disappointed that Georgie wouldn't be there.

As we climbed into the limousine, Celeste said, "Do you think there will be any terrifying growls and whizzing balls of light like there were at the séance at Barbara Watkins's mansion?" She could hardly contain her excitement.

"I'm sorry to disappoint you," I said, "but I don't think that will happen this time."

"Well, that will be a disappointment to quite a few people," she said, frowning.

"I'm sure there will be a few people happy if it *doesn't* happen," I replied, thinking of Irma Chavin and Dr. Plimpton.

"There will be a lot more people at the séance tonight," Celeste warned me. "And a lot more disappointment. The whole town is talking about it."

So much for avoiding bad publicity.

"How many people will Dr. Plimpton allow around the table?" I asked her.

"Oh, I think there will just be seven of us around the table, including you," she said. "But after the Watkins's séance, everybody we've talked to wants to attend this one. I told Marian McKelvie what was going on, and she said it wouldn't be a problem if more people showed up, but each of us could not have more than six guests. Marian checked with Dr. Plimpton, and he said he wasn't concerned how many came, but they could not be in the atrium during the séance."

"Where will they be?" I asked, puzzled.

"Oh, they'll still have a good view of the proceedings," said Celeste. "The McKelvies have large conservatories on each side of the atrium. Marian is so excited that she's hired extra waiters and staff to prepare food and serve at the event. It's going to be quite the shindig."

The magnificent McKelvie mansion was on a small, fifty-acre farm about ten minutes outside of London. Our limousine arrived at the sweeping front steps of the mansion about fifteen minutes prior to seven o'clock. It was a colonial mansion, not quite as imposing as the Watkins' residence, but a grand building in its own right. Soaring columns supported a pediment far overhead, the windows were open, and music emanated from within. Mrs. Bedgegood and I stepped out of the vehicle and were promptly greeted and escorted up the steps into the grand foyer by a footman. Marian McKelvie, who was waiting inside, smiled when she saw Celeste, shook my hand, smiled again, and said, "I'm glad the law is here. It saves me the trouble of hiring security."

As we made our way further into the house, we were offered champagne and canapés by servers dressed for a formal occasion. I declined the champagne but helped myself to the canapés. A live band was playing classical music at the end of a ballroom.

An older gentleman in a tuxedo with the smug, self-satisfied look of a man who knew his own worth, approached us. He was broad shouldered and slightly stooped, leaning heavily on a cane.

"Evening, Celeste," he said to Mrs. Bedgegood.

"Butch, this is—" Marian started, beginning to introduce us.

"Don't tell me his name," said Butch with a wave of his hand. "I won't remember. I've got too many names knocking around in this coconut already," he said, tapping the side of his head. "But it's good to meet you all the same, young man.

Have some champagne, have a good time. Celeste will show you around."

Butch shouted at someone behind us and hobbled off as abruptly as he'd appeared. Marian smiled apologetically. "Don't take it personally," she said. "He's like that with everyone."

"Everyone below a certain annual income," Celeste corrected her.

Marian grimaced good naturedly. "Well, I must be off. I've got more guests arriving."

Marian left us to attend to her duties as hostess, and I listened politely while Celeste chatted to several people she knew. I felt a tap on the shoulder, and when I turned, I found myself face to face with Chief Bedgegood. I almost choked on my shrimp.

"My wife and I are very pleased to be here," said the chief, slapping me on the shoulder. "This is quite an event." The woman beside him smiled. Though getting on in years, it was obvious that she had been quite a beauty in her youth. Her dress was dazzling. I was sorry Georgie couldn't be here to see it.

Before I could say anything in reply, his aunt Celeste said, "Bubbles! I'm so happy to see you here with your beautiful wife, Marilyn."

"It's good to see you, Auntie," Chief Bedgegood replied, putting his finger across his lips as she turned away from him, reminding me not to say a word about his pet name. "Or else," he whispered aloud.

I responded with the zipped-lip signal.

At that moment, someone said, "Attention please! Could I have everyone's attention!" There was a sharp rapping of metal on wood.

When I turned to see who was speaking, I saw it was Butch McKelvie. He was standing on a small portable podium, rapping the end of his cane on the boards. Once the crowd became quiet, Mr. McKelvie introduced Dr. Plimpton.

Dr. Plimpton took McKelvie's place on the podium. He thanked the people for coming and said there were printed cards available for anybody who wished to contact him about a future séance. Evidently, contrary to his fears, all this excitement had produced a good business opportunity for Dr. Plimpton.

Dr. Plimpton then said, "I would like you to follow in a procession behind myself and Mr. and Mrs. McKelvie as we proceed to the séance site."

There was a swell of murmuring and hushed exclamations of excitement as the doctor proceeded to lead us down a wide hall to the atrium area at the back of the house.

No inner room had been specially constructed for this séance. It wasn't necessary. The atrium at the back of the McKelvie mansion was a square rectangular space sixteen feet by sixteen feet. The atrium reached a height of about twenty-five feet. It was covered at the top by a square of four-foot-wide glass panels. As you walked through the open archway into the atrium, and looked up to the glass ceiling so far away, there was a wonderful sense of openness.

On each side of the atrium there were archways that led into conservatories, or indoor gardens. On the far side of the atrium, large doors, ten feet in height, opened onto a rear balcony with a magnificent view of the surrounding countryside. The setting was magical.

When everyone was assembled in the atrium, Dr. Plimpton spoke again: "The only people allowed in the atrium during the séance are the seven guests at the table, as well as me and my two helpers. The rest of you are to retire to the conservatories on the right and left, where seating has been arranged and where refreshments will be available. Please move to those areas now."

While the other guests took their seats, the furniture required for the séance, which had been distributed discreetly along the sides of the atrium, was now moved to the middle of the atrium floor. This séance table was in the shape of a heptagon. The seven of us took our places at the table while Dr. Plimpton took his place behind a pulpit. Next to the pulpit was a small table covered with a gold-coloured cloth. Carefully placed in the middle of this small table stood a Ouija board and a planchette. The lights were dimmed.

Using his oratorical voice, Dr. Plimpton spoke: "We will now join hands to demonstrate our unity of purpose and our common desire to communicate with the spiritual world. Tonight, we are using a table in the shape of the heptagon because a heptagon represents the seven days of creation and is a special symbol to ward off evil."

He clapped his hands sharply twice and his assistants, Simon and Simone, approached the séance table carrying a golden tray which held a single golden candleholder containing a purple candle glowing with a steady flame. As they had done at the previous séance, while Simon held the tray, Simone used the purple candle to light the white candles that were placed in front of each of us.

With the candles lit, Dr. Plimpton intoned, "The candle flames will dispel negative energy and herald the arrival of peace and truth and purity. We are now ready to summon the spiritual world in our search for wisdom and tranquility."

He closed his eyes and turned his head up toward the heavens beyond the glass of the atrium. There was a dramatic pause and then he opened his eyes and said, "I sense a channel is now open for communication. We will use a Ouija board and planchette as tools to facilitate our communication with the spirits. Mrs. Barbara Watkins will be the first seeker of knowledge."

Simone carefully placed the Ouija board and planchette in front of Barbara, who let go of her neighbours' hands and placed one hand upon the other on top of the planchette. Her neighbours placed their hands on her shoulders.

In a hesitant, tearful, cracking voice, Barbara Watkins asked, "Who killed my husband?"

It had been very quiet up to this point, but now it was even quieter. To everyone in the conservatories, with the exception of Chief Bedgegood, and everyone in the atrium, with the exception of me, this was revelatory. There had been nothing in the newspapers about the death of Roger Watkins.

The planchette began to move slowly across the Ouija board. It hovered between the letters A and B and stopped midway between them.

Barbara Watkins said very quietly, "The spirit says the answer is between A and B. I—I don't know what that means."

There was a murmur from the conservatories. Everyone was eager to know.

Dr. Plimpton said softly, but with a voice that carried, "The spirit is telling you there is an answer, and in time you will know it, but the time is not ripe. For the moment, it must remain hidden in that nether region between A and B." Then he asked, "Do you have another question, Mrs. Watkins?"

There was a pause while she regained her composure, and then she asked, "What was the motive?" This time the planchette guided her to the letter M and stopped.

Barbara Watkins gasped and said louder than she intended, "It was done for money!"

A susurration of whispers arose from the conservatories. Everyone had been listening intently, still stunned by the innocent announcement of Roger Watkins's death, but now that his wife, Barbara, had broken down into tears, the revelation threatened to disrupt the proceedings. Dr. Plimpton called a temporary halt to the séance.

In a soft voice, he asked Barbara if she would like to leave the séance, but she refused. "No, no, I'm alright," she insisted, blowing her nose on a handkerchief. "I won't ruin it for the others. We're united in common purpose."

When she had recovered sufficiently, Dr. Plimpton clapped his hands sharply twice and asked for silence. "We will continue. Please respect the spirits, please be quiet," he said.

When everyone had quieted, the séance resumed. The Ouija board and planchette were given to Alice Mulder, who asked about her daughter again. Her daughter's spirit assured her that she was happy and not angry at her mother or father.

When it was Irma Chavin's turn to summon the spirit world, she asked, in a hesitant voice, "Can I speak to my husband?"

The planchette under her hands began to move rapidly. Without ever quite leaving the board, it slid first to one end then the other, careening off each edge before sliding to the other. It did this over and over again, moving frantically and chaotically from edge to edge, until Irma, quite audibly distressed, hollered, "I can't let go of the planchette! What am I to do?"

Simone quickly came and placed her right hand on top of Irma's. The planchette slowed to a stop on the word NO. Irma fainted.

Simon caught Irma before she could slump to the floor, and, once again, the séance was interrupted by excited murmurs from the audience. Dr. Plimpton asked for quiet again. Irma recovered after a whiff of smelling salts, and one of her daughters came in from one of the conservatories and took her to another room where she could rest.

Dr. Plimpton intoned, "We are sorry for disturbing the spirits present tonight. Please don't abandon us. We still have many questions."

He observed the empty chair at the table and said, "We must complete the circle. Would anyone like to fill the vacant space?"

Chief Bedgegood's wife, Marilyn, stood, glittering in her dress, and was quickly welcomed to the circle. Simon relit Irma's candle, which had been extinguished during the commotion, and the séance resumed.

The rest of the séance was relatively uneventful.

When it was my turn to operate the planchette, in an effort to lighten the mood, I asked, "Will the baby my wife and I are expecting be a boy or girl?"

This received an amused murmur from the audience.

I felt the planchette moving under my hands, which surprised me because I was quite certain I hadn't moved it myself, and it stopped at the letter B. Marilyn Bedgegood, who was sitting beside me, blurted, "Congratulations, Joel, it's a boy!"

Laughter filled the conservatories. Even Dr. Plimpton smiled.

Dr. Plimpton thanked the spirits and then thanked everyone in attendance for their cooperation. He announced, "The séance for this evening has been completed."

At that point, everyone began to speak, drinks were quickly served, the band began playing again, and the séance turned into a cocktail party. For the next hour, there was conversation and laughter, aside from the odd tear when Irma Chavin returned to the party.

Once more, I found myself face to face with Chief Bedgegood. He had been a firm nonbeliever of the spirit world, but tonight's séance had left him wondering if there wasn't something to it. Our conversation was interrupted when one of the waiters tapped me on the shoulder and said there was a gentleman at the door who wished to speak to me.

I followed the young waiter to the door. "It's a policeman, sir," said the waiter. "He's waiting outside. He told me not to let anyone know the police were here except for you. His name is Insp. Simpson."

"Thank you," I said and stepped out onto the front portico.

"Over here," said a soft voice from the shadows at the edge of the light.

I walked over and found the inspector hiding behind a pillar.

"You were right to be suspicious about tonight's séance, Joel," said Insp. Simpson. "We spotted someone leaving through a side door of the premises with a large carrying case. We watched him carry it to a 1937 Ford delivery van with the words Garber's Bakery painted on the side. He opened the back door of the van, and then he and an accomplice, who was already inside the van, appeared to empty the contents of the case into the back of the van. The suspect returned to the house. We decided to wait to see what happened next. We weren't disappointed. Within fifteen minutes, he made a return trip to the van with another full case of goods.

"Just as they finished emptying the case a second time, I had two of my men move in. The constables made certain they weren't armed, and then relieved them of the keys to the van. They weren't happy to see us. There's quite a collection of antiques in the back of the van."

"Where are the men now?" I asked.

"I have them in separate patrol cars. But it's not two men. The man's in the back of my car, and his accomplice, a woman, is in the back of another car. I haven't interviewed them yet; I thought you might be interested in seeing them first."

I had my suspicions about who the accomplice was. "I'd like to see the woman first," I said.

Insp. Simpson led me down a path, over a slight embankment, and through a line of pine trees to a small, graveled parking area that was remote from the mansion. On this side of the trees, the light from the mansion was almost completely blocked. A dark shape blocking the stars showed the outline of a large building at the edge of the gravel. I inhaled the familiar aroma of manure.

"This is a great location," I said, looking around. "No one can see you from the house or from the area where most of the cars are parked. How did you find this spot?"

"You told me the chief wanted to keep this low profile, so we knew we had to find a good hiding spot for the cars. One of the men on my squad has been to the McKelvie estate before. His dad is a veterinarian, and he helps his dad occasionally. The McKelvies have a lot of expensive purebred horses. This new farm building we're parked next to is a riding hall."

He turned on a flashlight and waved the beam over the side of the building. It looked like an enormous barn. You could have fit my entire block on Princess Ave. inside of it. I gave Insp. Simpson a puzzled look.

"Don't feel bad," he said. "I didn't know what it meant either. I made the mistake and asked the constable. I found out. I also got a half hour lecture on equestrian events." Insp. Simpson chuckled and said, "I'll keep it simple for you: it's a covered paddock where you can train your horses for show events."

I shook my head. It was the kind of thing that made you realize that people like McKelvie, and people like me, inhabited two completely different worlds.

By the light of the flashlight, Insp. Simpson and I walked over to the patrol car where the woman was being held. A constable waiting there greeted us.

I leaned over and peeked through the slightly lowered rear seat window at the person inside. "Hello, Sarah," I said.

The woman gasped. I had caught her totally unaware. She stared at me, speechless.

"You must've left Celeste Bedgegood's house early tonight," I said, just to further convince her that I knew who she was.

She turned away, clenching her jaw.

"Insp. Simpson just informed me that he caught the two of you taking antiques from the McKelvie estate," I said. "I haven't met the other thief yet, but I'm willing to bet his name is Connor McDougall."

"You'll never understand," Sarah spat, turning back to me. "All those people in there, holding their silly séances, throwing their money around, while other people have to do without. They have so much, and I have so little. I'm practically starving. With my husband locked up, I was getting desperate."

"Sounds like a bunch of excuses to me," I said. "Most people don't have any more than you do, Sarah, if they have as much, but they're not going around breaking the law. And starving people steal food, not antiques."

"Spoken like a real cop," Sarah said with a sneer.

"I think you're working for somebody," I said, ignoring her jab. "Do you want to tell me who it is?"

Sarah didn't answer me, she just gave me the evil eye.

"If you cooperate with me and tell me who's behind this robbery—and, I suspect, several other robberies—then I'll make certain that I tell the judge about your cooperation, and you'll get a more lenient sentence. You think about that while I talk to your accomplice."

I walked over to Insp. Simpson's car. Simpson opened the back door of his police cruiser and said gruffly, "Det. Joel Franklin would like to speak to you. Mind your manners."

Four of Insp. Simpson's squad members were standing near the car, so I didn't anticipate a problem.

"We haven't met," I said, leaning over the open door, "but I believe your name is Connor McDougall."

"Did she tell you that?" said the man inside, who was dressed like a delivery man. He was in need of a shave, smelled faintly of booze, and was missing a tooth.

"No, she didn't tell me your name or anything else. I'm a detective; it's my job to know these things," I said.

He gave me a strange look and said, "Yeah, I'm Connor."

I stared back at him for a moment. Finally, I said, "I'm not sure how many years you want to spend in prison, Connor, but I have a little bit of control over how long you'll be locked up. It's called 'You help me, and I'll help you.' If you give me a lot of help, then I'll explain to the judge that you're a good person who just did a bad thing, and that you'd like to make amends. He will be impressed, and your sentence will be much shorter than it would be otherwise."

The man muttered under his breath. "What would you like to know?" he said.

"I think I know most of what's gone on already," I said, "but I do need you to confirm it as a witness. Tell me how you are contacted, who contacts you, and how many of these robberies you've committed."

"My partner Sarah receives a phone call from Garber's Bakery at Celeste Bedgegood's home. During the phone call, Sarah is informed where the van will be parked, what address we're going to, and what time we're supposed to be there. When we get in the van, there's always a set of instructions. It's usually a map of the house showing us what rooms to go to, and a list of what we're supposed to steal from the room. The map also shows us which doors will be unlocked."

"Who phones Sarah?" I asked.

"Someone called Marguerite. I've never met her," said Connor. "I've never talked to her. You'll have to talk to Sarah about her."

"How many robberies have you done using this arrangement?" I asked.

"This is the fifth one," said Connor.

"So, you've robbed every house where a séance is taking place?" I asked.

Connor shrugged.

"Who's the mastermind behind these robberies?" I asked.

"I don't know. But since we've been committing these during the séances, I assume it's Dr. Plimpton," said Connor. "But I don't know for certain. I can't swear to it."

"Thank you, Connor," I said, and I stepped away from the car and motioned for Insp. Simpson to join me.

"Here's the plan," I said to the inspector. "I want Sarah taken downtown and booked. I can talk to her later. I want you to help Connor deliver the van and its contents to wherever it's supposed to be parked. Keep it under surveillance, and when they come to pick it up, arrest whoever appears and bring them down to the station."

"With pleasure," said the inspector.

Thursday, June 22nd

I got up earlier Thursday than I anticipated, abruptly wakened from a sound sleep by Georgie a little after two in the morning. She was tugging violently on my arm, crying, "It's time, Joel! It's time to go!"

"Where?" I said stupidly, not even half awake.

"To Victoria Hospital!" she all but screamed.

She winced and held her stomach, breathing sharply. "We have to go now!" she said, her voice rising an octave.

Realization finally dawned on me, jolting me from my groggy state. I'm slow, but I get there eventually.

I jumped out of bed and fumbled around in the semi-darkness for my clothes.

"I started having contractions about an hour ago," said Georgie, throwing a pair of pants at me. "They're about seven or eight minutes apart now."

"What about Annie?" I said, almost falling over as I caught my foot in my pant leg.

"I telephoned Kay five minutes ago," said Georgie, trying to get her feet in a pair of slippers. "I told her to just come over, the front door would be open. I think I hear her now."

As if on cue, we heard a "Hallo!" from downstairs.

I helped Georgie down the stairs, almost stumbling but catching myself. Kay pressed herself up against the wall as we passed her out the door.

"Good luck!" she called out to us as we waddled toward the car.

ONE MAN LEFT

It only took us about twenty minutes to get to the emergency entrance at Victoria Hospital. The one blessing of having contractions in the middle of the night was the absence of traffic. During the trip, Georgie kept saying, "Hurry, hurry, hurry!" and "Don't stop, there's no one coming!" at every intersection.

I wanted to get there as badly as she did. I might be a good detective, but I knew I'd be a lousy obstetrician. Fortunately, we made it to the hospital before my services as a doctor were required.

I helped Georgie hobble inside and they quickly put her on a gurney. They wheeled her up behind two other women on gurneys, who were also close to delivering. There were uniformed nurses hovering around the three women, timing their contractions, and telling them to breathe. The delivery room door opened, and a smiling woman with a squalling baby was wheeled out. The nurses grabbed the second gurney in line and said, "This one's next! Her contractions are down under a minute. That baby will be here by the time she's in the delivery room." Wheels squeaking, they raced her away.

I held Georgie's hand while we waited. Though it couldn't have been more than twenty minutes, it felt like hours. When it was Georgie's turn to be wheeled into the delivery room, one of the nurses detached me from the gurney, took hold of my elbow, and pointed me to the waiting room.

"Right over here, Dad," she said.

Still in a daze, I saw other men, probably dads like me, pacing and sitting hunched over in chairs. I slumped into a chair by the door and closed my eyes.

It seemed like weeks, but it was only forty-five minutes later that our doctor came to the waiting room and said, "Congratulations, Joel! You have strong, healthy little boy. Eight pounds, two ounces. Both mother and son are fine."

"That's wonderful," I said, louder than I should have. I jumped up and vigorously pumped the doctor's hand. "I owe you a cigar."

"You can go and see them now," he said, smiling. "They're just down the hall in the recovery room."

I all but ran down the hall, having no real idea where I was going. A nurse stopped me and said, "Are you Joel?"

I nodded.

"Right this way," she said, steering me into a room with several recovering mothers. "Your wife and the baby will be in the hospital for a week," said the nurse as we approached the bed. "Do you have any other children that need to be looked after?"

For a moment, I drew a blank. Then Annie's face appeared before me, indignant. "Annie!" I was so concerned about Georgie and the baby that I'd forgotten all about her.

"Yes, one," I clarified. "Kay's with her. Kay's our friend."

The nurse nodded and led me over to the bed. Georgie, wearing the biggest smile I had ever seen, was holding onto our new son. He was bundled in a little blue blanket, his soft pink face splendidly tranquil.

"Now we have to pick out a name," Georgie said quietly. "We are not going to call him Junior any longer. I think we should call him Arthur Edward. Arthur is your dad's first name, and Edward is my dad's second name."

"I like it," I said, leaning in close to them. "Arthur Edward Franklin sounds like the name of a caring, clever man."

After admiring our new son for a couple of minutes, I said, "The nurse told me that you and Arthur will be in the hospital for a week. I guess I should find someone to help with Annie. We can't ask Kay—"

"That's all been taken care of, Joel," said Georgie serenely. "One call to my mother, and she'll be here in a couple of hours."

"What about your dad?" I said. Ethel, Georgie's mother, had to watch Garth almost every minute of the day because of his dementia.

"My cousin Mary is a nurse, and her husband, Charlie, has a week's vacation. They told my mom they would come over and stay in the house and look after my dad until she came home. They just have one boy, Randy, and he's fifteen and in Grade 10 at CHS. Randy doesn't mind because his best friend Jeff just moved a block away from my mom and dad's, and now they can walk to school together."

"Your cousin's a gem, but does she know what she's in for?"

"It's her specialty, working with people with dementia," said Georgie. "So go home and make all those important telephone calls. The first one is to my mom, and the next one is to your mom and dad."

It was just after five o'clock in the morning when I got home. When I opened the front door, Annie raced down the stairs from her bedroom and began looking around. "Where is it?" she said.

Kay came out of the kitchen. "There's a hot coffee in the kitchen for you, Joel," she said, smiling wearily. "While you drink your coffee, you can tell us all the news."

As I walked to the kitchen, Annie tugged my hand and jumped up and down, saying, "Where is it, Daddy? Do I have a sister, or do I have a brother?"

"Mommy and your little baby brother are still at the hospital," I said.

By the time I had told Annie and Kay about Mommy and the new baby, and had made my telephone calls to Chaseford, it was after seven o'clock in the morning. Georgie's mom, Ethel, was so excited that she broke down and cried on the phone. My mother was just as happy.

"Georgie's mom said she would be here by suppertime," I told Kay.

"That's not a problem. I'll be glad to look after Annie until Ethel arrives," she said. "We're going to make this place look special for Mommy and Arthur Edward, aren't we, Annie?"

Annie could barely restrain her excitement.

I made two stops on my way to the police station. First, I went to the local bakeshop and bought two dozen doughnuts, then I stopped at the United Cigar store and purchased two boxes of good cigars. With these supplies, I knew I was ready to brag about my baby boy when I arrived at work.

By ten o'clock, all my doughnuts and cigars were gone, and I'd received an abundance of congratulatory messages. Even the chief had complimented me on my choice of cigar.

I was surprised that I hadn't seen Insp. Simpson. I thought he might be the first person to come see me; not to congratulate me on the birth of my son, but to bring me the exciting news that they had taken someone into custody.

I went hunting for the inspector. I didn't find him, but I found one of the members of his team, Kevin Broadman. "Where's Insp. Simpson?" I asked.

"He's over at the fairgrounds checking on the van. No one has come for it yet," said Cst. Broadman.

"Thanks," I said, disappointed. I checked the time on my watch. "I'm going to interview Sarah Olson, the woman we picked up last night who was stealing antiques from the McKelvies. If your boss appears, let him know I was looking for him."

When Sarah Olson arrived at the interview room, her haughty attitude of the previous evening had disappeared. Hair uncombed, dark circles under her eyes, she was in a state of mild disarray. Spending the night in a jail cell can do that to you.

"I'm hoping you can help me, Sarah," I said coolly when she'd seated herself across the table from me. "Connor was somewhat cooperative. He told me that someone named Marguerite contacts you by telephone at Celeste Bedgegood's home. Marguerite tells you where the Garber's Bakery van will be parked. When you and Connor pick up the van, instructions for the theft are in a folder on the front seat."

"Connor told you all that?" she said in a tone of disbelief. "He told me to keep my mouth shut!"

"Well, when I told Connor that if he helped me, I would help him, and that the judge would go easier on him when it came to sentencing, he was very forthcoming," I said, smiling slightly. "Did Connor tell me the truth?"

I could see from her expression that she had decided to cooperate with me too. "Will you speak to the judge on my behalf too?" she asked.

"Certainly," I said.

"Everything Connor told you is true," she said quickly, as if afraid I might change my mind.

"How did Marguerite get in touch with you in the first place?" I asked.

"One morning, a couple months ago, when I answered the telephone at Mrs. Bedgegood's, a woman on the other end of the line asked to speak to Sarah Olson. I said, 'You're talking to her.' I was surprised because no one ever calls for me there. She said her name was Marguerite, and she would like to meet me to discuss a business proposition. I thought it smelled fishy right away. What kind of business could a poor housekeeper help her with? But I asked her, 'What kind of business?' She said, 'You'll be stealing antiques.' I said, 'I'm no gangster, Miss, I'm a housekeeper.' She thought that was funny and laughed. She said, 'Don't worry, it's safe. No weapons involved, just a little discretion. It will be very lucrative.'

"I was down in my luck, and I was getting tired of listening to Celeste Bedgegood complaining about the poor job I was doing. Nothing is ever good enough for her. I thought, 'If I can make a bit of money, I can quit this job and move to a different city. Somewhere my husband can't find me when he gets out of prison, and where I won't have to listen to Mrs. Bedgegood anymore.'

"So I told Marguerite I might be interested. She set up a meeting with me at Bing's Diner on Richmond Street for ten o'clock the next morning. Marguerite said she'd never met me before—she'd heard about me through a mutual acquaintance—so she told me to wear a hat with a pink ribbon pinned to the side of it.

"I was at Bing's Diner at ten o'clock with the hat and ribbon. I waited for fifteen minutes, and nobody appeared, so I got up and left. As soon as I walked out the door, this woman with long blonde hair—it looked like a wig to me—approached and said, 'You must be Sarah Olson.'

"I nodded and she said, 'I'm sorry you had to wait, but I wanted to make certain I could trust you. If you're going to work for us, you need to be able to do what you're told.' I looked around and said, 'Us? I don't see nobody else.' 'You won't,' she said, with a kind of a sly look. 'We're very good.'

"The way she said that kind of frightened me. I thought everyone on the street was working for her. I'm even a little worried talking about it now."

"What happened next?" I asked.

"We walked further down Richmond Street and went into another diner. She told me to order whatever I wanted. Then she said to me, 'Are you committed to this, Sarah?' I said, 'Yes.' Then Marguerite said, 'I think you're ready for the next step. You need to find a partner you can trust to help you carry out these thefts. At least one of you will have to be able to drive a delivery van. Your partner will never meet me, and you will never meet me face to face again. From this point on, your instructions will be over the telephone, or you'll find them in an envelope at the location we give you. You will be well paid.'

"When Marguerite said this, she handed me an envelope with money in it. 'This is your hiring bonus,' she said. 'If you wish to share some of this with your partner, that's your business. Consider yourself hired. You have one week to find a partner. You will receive a telephone call ten days from now. Stay until you've finished your order, then leave.'

"As soon as she left, I counted the money. Under the table so no one would see me. There was $400 in that envelope. I'd never seen so much money. I finished my pie and left and then got in touch with Connor. He agreed to be my partner, and, ten days from the date of my meeting with Marguerite, I got the first phone call."

Sarah was now shaking. She really was scared. She was no hardened criminal.

"We can protect you, Sarah," I said.

"I hated my husband for being a criminal, and now I'm no better than he is," she said and started to cry.

I waited a minute for her to regain her composure, then I said, "I want you to think for a minute or two, Sarah, and then I want you to describe Marguerite to me as best you can."

Sarah wiped her cheeks and then sat and thought.

"She was almost as tall as I am because, when she came up to me on the sidewalk, we were pretty much eye to eye. That would make her about five feet, six inches. I don't know what colour her hair is; I'm sure she was wearing a wig when she talked to me. But her eyes weren't quite blue; they were kind of greenish. I remember because it's an unusual colour. She was of average build, sort of pretty, and not much more than thirty years old; maybe a little older, but definitely not older than forty. One thing I'll never forget is her voice or the way she talked. But I don't think I can describe it to you. It was just ... different. Like she was biting all her words."

"That's a good description," I said, jotting everything down. "That's helpful. I'll be sure the judge knows how cooperative you're being."

Actually, I was disappointed. She had given me a good description, but it wasn't a description that would fit Simone, one of Dr. Plimpton's assistants. Simone, at the most, was five feet tall, and very soft spoken. It was hard to imagine her as an imposing presence that would intimidate the likes of Sarah Olson. I was still pretty much convinced that Dr. Plimpton was involved in this somehow, but this new lead was pointing in the wrong direction.

I had one more important task ahead of me before I went home for supper. I knew Georgie's mom, Ethel, and my daughter, Annie, would want a report on Georgie and the baby, so I went to Victoria Hospital to visit my wife and my new son, Arthur Edward.

Little Arthur Edward was sleeping, as peaceful as a cherub, and Georgie was half asleep. I gave her a kiss and we whispered a little, but I didn't stay long. She was too exhausted.

I hadn't seen Ethel for a couple months, and I was shocked when I got home for supper. Ethel looked ten years older than she had the last time I'd seen her. Dealing with Garth had drained her. However, she welcomed me with a big smile and a warm hug. She was ecstatic about her new grandson, and she was delighted to spend some time with her granddaughter Annie. I think she was also happy to have a vacation from Garth, though she would never have said so.

Grandma Ethel could hardly wait for me to finish my supper. Ethel and I were going to the hospital this evening to visit Georgie and see the baby. Annie was pouting; she was very disappointed that she couldn't go with us. Ethel and I tried to explain to her that the hospital had rules, and that she wasn't nearly old enough to visit someone in the hospital, even her mommy. Annie brightened up a bit when I told her that Auntie Kay was coming over to stay with her.

In a flash of inspiration, Annie asked, "Can Teddy go to the hospital?" referring to her favourite teddy bear.

"Yes, Teddy can go," I said. "Hospitals make exceptions for teddy bears."

Annie was thrilled. "You can take Teddy," she said, "and Teddy can see Baby Rfur!"

How could I argue with that?

Friday, June 23rd

This morning, when I got down to the breakfast table, Ethel seemed to be somewhat relaxed.

"Did you have a comfortable night?" I asked. Auntie Kay had made up the spare bedroom for her, but the bed didn't have the most comfortable mattress.

"I did," she replied, looking a little guilty. "It took me a while to get used to the fact that Garth wasn't in the house. I'm so used to listening for him. I suppose you know I have to lock him in his room at night so he doesn't go wandering off or get into trouble."

I looked at her sympathetically, thinking about what a strong woman she had to be to have been doing this for a couple of years now. I could see where Georgie got her strength. Ethel was determined not to give up on Garth, so I chose my words carefully.

"Someday, Garth's going to have to go into a special home or a hospital," I said.

"I know," Ethel said, wiping a tear from her eye. "But I'm just so worried he won't be treated right. He can cause a lot of aggravation. Sometimes I think he's not the same person I married."

I poured each of us some coffee.

"Have you talked to anybody about getting him into the Chaseford Home for the Aged?" I asked.

"Yes, Georgie and I have talked about this with my niece Mary," said Ethel, colouring a little. "Mary has worked with some dementia patients, and she's looking after Garth for the next week or so, so she will be able to tell by the end of the week whether he will be a fit for the Chaseford Home for the Aged. I just hate it so."

"We all need help, sometimes," I said consolingly. "There's no shame in that."

As I made my way to the desk in the detective department of the station, I received a fresh round of congratulatory comments. Someone asked me when the next one was coming, and everyone laughed. I enjoyed the attention. I was the proud Papa. When I arrived at my desk, there was a note on it.

The note was from my superior officer, Insp. O'Neill. It read:

Sarah Olson wants to speak to you

I thought I'd visit Insp. O'Neill's office first to see if he knew what Sarah wanted before I went to see her. He wasn't there, so I just made my way over to the jail.

I found a free interview room and had Sarah escorted there. When she arrived, I noticed once again that jail didn't agree with her. She looked even worse than last time.

"Sarah, I received a note that you wanted to see me," I said, sitting down across from her. "Did you forget to tell me something yesterday?"

"Last night, I thought over what I told you and remembered something else," said Sarah. "I don't know whether it's important or not, but every time after we completed a robbery, the next day I always got a phone call from Marguerite. She always asked me the same question. 'Did you get the goods?' I'd say, 'Yes,' and she would hang up. I just realized last night that maybe that was her way of checking to see whether Connor and I had been apprehended. I'm sorry I forgot to mention it yesterday, it just slipped my mind."

"That's good information, Sarah," I said, concealing my irritation. It would have been nice if she'd mentioned it sooner, but I didn't think she'd hid it on purpose. "If you continue being this helpful, I'll be able to make a very good report to the judge on your behalf."

She was visibly relieved that I wasn't angry with her.

Now what? I thought after she'd been taken back to her cell. This was going to be a little more time consuming than I'd hoped. I figured I'd better get a hold of Insp. Simpson and let him know that he should call off the surveillance.

I was going to have to do some of that 'tough slogging,' as Chief Petrovic always used to say when I was a constable in Chaseford. Chief Petrovic reminded us constantly that the persistent chasing down of information, no matter how boring a routine it may seem, was what usually cracked a case. You couldn't find that missing puzzle piece without looking under all the furniture.

Now that we had the van, we we're going to have to do some checking to determine who the current owner was. That would be a lot easier if we had the registration. It would be a lot harder if all we had was a factory number. We'd also have to have the owners of the five homes where séances took place interviewed to produce a list of stolen properties. Once we had that list, we could talk to pawnshops or auctioneers or other people that might deal with those goods. Hopefully, we'd get lucky.

When I got to my desk, I found another note. This one read:

Barbara Watkins has the key to the menagerie??

I smiled to myself, imagining the confusion of the person who took the message.

I picked up the phone and called Barbara Watkins's number. The butler, Jason, answered. He informed me that Mrs. Watkins was not taking calls, but that he was expecting my call, and that I could come by that afternoon to see the locked room. I thanked him and hung up. This was one piece of the puzzle that I really wanted to look at.

On my way out the door, I ran into Insp. O'Neill.

"Where's the fire?" he said.

I stopped, suddenly recalling that I needed to speak to Insp. Simpson.

"Could you do me a favour and get a hold of Insp. Simpson?" I said. "Tell him to call off the surveillance on the van. I'll explain when I get back."

Rodney led me down to the cellar and escorted me to the door of the 'menagerie.'

"Mrs. Watkins got the key with Mr. Watkins's personal effects," said Rodeny, unlocking the door. "I'm supposed to accompany you, but if it's alright with you, Detective, I'll wait out here."

"That will be fine, Rodney, thanks."

I opened the door. I wasn't sure what to expect, but I sure wasn't expecting a tiger to leap out at me when I turned on the lights.

When my heart stopped trying to burst its way out of my chest, I realized that I was face to face with the tiger that had almost killed Roger Watkins. Or rather, with the stuffed skin of that tiger posed in the middle of a fearsome attack. No wonder Barbara had asked him to move it.

I drew nearer—not quite convinced it was dead—and gave it a closer inspection. The teeth and the claws were truly terrifying up close, and I felt new respect for the man who could survive its attack. The eyes, though made of glass, were especially riveting. They seemed to follow you wherever you went. I could understand why Rodney didn't like being left alone in the room with it.

I had a vivid recollection of the sounds I'd heard at the séance and wondered. Could it be ...? I shook my head, smiling to myself. No, the idea was just too preposterous.

I turned my attention to the other displays in Mr. Watkins's collection. Among them I found three types of deer or antelope—they weren't named, so I wasn't sure what they were—a warthog; several large birds, including an ostrich; a branch adorned with several small monkeys; a python looped around another branch; and a crocodile with wide open jaws. There were also a number of very impressive fish attached to mounts and framed collections of butterflies and other insects behind glass. A number of cabinets with glass windows displayed other odd curios, mostly rocks, fossils, carvings, primitive jewellery, and pottery. What I didn't find was any evidence of a crime. My curiosity had been satisfied, but my search hadn't progressed the investigation.

On my way toward the door, I noticed something by the wall, just behind the base of one of the animals. A rat trap.

"Rodney, do you have a problem with rats in here?" I asked.

Rodney blushed a little. "We've spotted a couple," he said. "They seem to like the animals. Mr. Watkins had me put down traps, but we don't catch very many."

"Do you ever use poison?"

"You mean rat poison? Yes, there's some in the workroom," he said.

"Thanks, Rodney. I think I'm done here."

Monday, June 26th

Saturday and Sunday had been a hectic two days. People had dropped into our home on Princess Ave. on their way to Victoria Hospital, while others had dropped in for a minute on their way back out of town. Many brought gifts, especially food, though there were blankets and toys and other things for the baby. Jay and Sylvia came with their children; Brad, who was seven, and Julie, who was just about to turn three. Georgie and I had both grown up in Chaseford, so that's where most of the people had come from, although we did get visits from some of our London friends. On hearing the news, Gwen and Alfred had cut short their honeymoon by a day, and after visiting Georgie and Arthur Edward in the hospital, spent most of Saturday helping Grandma Ethel and me take care of our guests. There were still plenty of leftovers for Sunday.

I was especially surprised and pleased when Chief Bedgegood and his wife showed up at the hospital for a visit Sunday evening. They had come to visit his wife's sister, who was recovering from an operation, and decided to stop by the maternity ward. They had brought Chief Bedgegood's aunt Celeste with them.

"You have a beautiful boy, Detective," Celeste had said to me, patting my arm and smiling. "It's a good thing he takes after Georgie."

I had chuckled uncertainly. I was sure she was kidding. Or at least hoped that she was.

"By the way," Celeste had then said, drawing me aside. "My housekeeper Sarah Olson seems to be missing. You can imagine my surprise when I called for her the other morning and she didn't appear. Your chief said to ask you about it."

I had glanced over at Chief Bedgegood, who had given me a wry smile.

"I'm sorry," I'd said, "but Sarah encountered some ... legal difficulties. She won't be returning as your employee any time soon."

"Ah, I see," Celeste had said with a wink. "And you can't tell me why because there's an investigation underway. That's what Bubbles always says. Not that you need to be a detective to figure this one out."

I made it!

I all but shouted it when I left my house Monday morning.

I had survived a weekend of a house full of relatives and friends. Much as I appreciated their congratulations and good wishes, there seemed to be few things as exhausting as a constant coming and going of people. Annie loved it, of course, because she got oodles of extra attention. Everywhere she turned there were smiling faces delighted to hear the story about Teddy's visit to the hospital to see Baby Rfur. I think Grandma Ethel enjoyed it a lot too. She didn't get out of the house much these days.

Once I was back at my desk at the police station, reality set in. I realized I was faced with two major investigations that I hadn't made a lot of progress on, and the euphoria of being a new dad quickly wore off.

I needed to get organized if I was going to get back on track. To get the information I required to solve the string of antique robberies, I knew I'd need a couple of extra sets of eyes and hands. I went and had a talk with Insp. O'Neill and convinced him to lend me two or three of his constables. I was frustrated by my lack of progress in my investigation of the murders of Roger Watkins and Edward Chavin, but it wasn't yet clear what my next step would be.

Once I had the blessing of the inspector, I quickly rounded up Csts. Carmichael and Johnson.

"Cst. Johnson, I need you to comb through some records for me," I said. "I want you to find out everything you can about that van. Start with the licence plate. If that doesn't do it, you might have to find the engine or factory number and do a bit of digging. The boys in the shop can help you with that."

"Yes sir."

"Cst. Carmichael, I want you to grab another constable, and, as soon as possible, I want the two of you out there conducting interviews of the six women holding the séances. Not all of them have held séances, but I want all of them interviewed. I want a list of all the items that may have been stolen from their places."

"If you'll refresh my memory, sir," said Cst. Carmichael, "who am I to contact?"

The original séance member interviews the night of Edward Chavin's death had been split between the constables, so Carmichael hadn't met them all yet.

"You'll need to interview Celeste Bedgegood, Barbara Watkins, Alice and Jordan Mulder, Marian and Butch McKelvie, Martha and Arthur Brightman, and Irma Chavin. I have a copy of the list here."

I handed him the list.

"Thank you, sir. I'll get to it right away."

Carmichael and Johnson left. I knew I might not have any new information from them for a day or two, so I needed to do some more serious thinking about those murders. I had to take the puzzle pieces I already had and try to fit them together. I decided to start with the murder of Roger Watkins.

I took out a pad of paper and started by jotting down what information I had about the death of Roger Watkins. From the autopsy, I noted:

> *The severe acid burns to Roger's face had most likely caused him to be instantly blinded*
>
> *There were three stab wounds; the third wound pierced his heart; death came quickly*
>
> *A small scrap of material, most likely from a shirt or the lining of a jacket, was recovered from Roger's clenched right fist*
>
> *The bottle, or container, holding the acid has not been recovered*
>
> *The murder weapon has not been recovered*

Then I added information that I had obtained from my exchange with Roger Watkins's essence:

> *He was murdered in his cellar office*
>
> *He didn't see his attacker*

ONE MAN LEFT

He was working on some documents

The body was likely taken out the back cellar hatchway door

Then I added some of my own conclusions:

His attacker seemed familiar with the office and the layout of the cellar—he (or she) knew where to hide to avoid being detected before the crime, and how to get the body out of the cellar without being observed

Meaning that the attacker was most likely one of the members of the board of the Group of Six Investments company, an employee, or a relative

Just as I finished the last sentence, I broke my pencil. It was only a stub, so I reached into the rarely used bottom drawer of my desk to pull out the box that contained my 2B graphite pencils. I was startled to see the eye of the amulet staring up at me.

I had received the amulet just after Christmas last year from Dr. Alfred Khryscoff, who had received it from a patient at the Ontario Hospital on Highbury Ave. The patient claimed that the amulet spoke to her, but as the patient had significant mental health problems, and a tenuous grasp on reality, she and the doctor jointly decided that the amulet was too dangerous for her to keep. Dr. Khryscoff told her of my interest in the occult, and when she met me, she said she wanted me to have the amulet.

In February, I had the amulet examined by Dr. Asim Arafe, an Egyptologist from the Royal Ontario Museum, and a friend of Dr. Khryscoff. He declared it a genuine artifact, probably at least 4,000 years old. He suggested that, in his expert opinion, the symbol on it was likely the Eye of Horus, sometimes known as the "All-Seeing Eye." Dr. Arafe and Dr. Khryscoff, both staunch men of science, thought it merely an interesting artifact. I knew better.

The amulet certainly didn't talk to me, as it had to its previous owner, but I was convinced it enhanced the abilities I already had. Unfortunately, the amulet also had a habit of inflicting distressing visions on me. I wasn't sure if the visions were of real events taking place now in the present, events of the past or future, or merely disturbing fantasies. In any case, I only used it for emergencies, and after returning from the island in Georgian Bay where we'd gone to rescue Dr. Khryscoff, I'd tossed the amulet in the bottom drawer of my desk. I'd needed a break.

But now I needed a different kind of break: a break in the case.

So, for the first time in two months, I picked up the amulet by the attached chain and looped it around my neck. I tucked the amulet under my shirt. So far so good; no disturbing visions.

I looked up at the clock. It was time for me to go and take another look at the location where the body had been found on the banks of the Thames. Perhaps I'd have something to add to my notes when I returned.

ONE MAN LEFT

It had been almost a week since Roger Watkins's body had been discovered in the shallow gravesite that I was standing over. The area had been cordoned off, and there was a sign that read:

CRIME SITE
DO NOT TRESSPASS
LONDON POLICE FORCE

I was pleased to note that the area looked relatively undisturbed. The Jensens, who owned the property, had quite understandably decided to go on vacation. On such a beautiful summer day, in such peaceful surroundings, with the mellow Thames burbling past and birds twittering in the trees, it was hard to believe I was looking at the scene of a tragedy.

I looked around to make sure I was alone, then lifted the amulet out from under my shirt and held it in my left hand. Its worn surface glinted dully in the light. If you held it just right, you could almost make out the symbols around the Eye. I closed my eyes and concentrated. I thought of Roger Watkins and a knife.

I felt a twitch in my right hand. It could've been anything, a muscle spasm, a mild case of nerves, but I opened my eyes and turned to my right. About fifteen feet away I saw a group of four cedar trees. They were perhaps five feet from the edge of the river.

I walked over to the cluster of cedars and got down my hands and knees so I could take a close look at the ground around the roots of the trees. That's when I spotted the knife.

It was just a faint gleam, a small part of the metal exposed to a stray beam of afternoon sunlight filtering down through the leaves. It looked like whoever had killed Roger Watkins had been in too much of a hurry to bury it and had just tossed it in among the trees. But why not toss it in the river? It was close to the water's edge; perhaps they'd tried to and missed. They must have been spooked.

I picked the knife up carefully using a handkerchief, in case there were prints on it, and placed it in the paper bag I had brought along on the off chance that I found something. I didn't know much about knives, but to my inexpert eye it appeared to be a bowie knife.

On the walk back to the car, I felt a sudden jolt, and the sky dimmed, as if the sun had been swallowed up by clouds. I felt dizzy and stumbled and had to lean against a tree to keep from falling. A rhythmic clanging, banging, clattering sound filled my ears, as if I were in a factory surrounded by running machinery, and I had a distinct vision of rows of gleaming metal casings rolling past, like the shells of huge bullets. I didn't know what I was being given a vision of, but I didn't like it. Reaching inside my shirt, I grabbed the Eye of Horus by the chain and yanked it off over my head. The amulet was going back in the drawer of my desk as soon as I got back to the station.

Wednesday, June 28th

I got a call just after nine o'clock Wednesday morning. "I don't believe it, Joel," said the voice on the telephone. It was Dick Robinson, the coroner.

"What is it that you don't believe, Dick?"

"Well, two things," he said. "I don't believe the lab guy was able to get prints off that knife you found—and, for the record, it is a bowie knife—the other thing that surprised me, though maybe it shouldn't, is that the prints on the knife are the same as the second set of prints we found on the pocket flask that contained the poison that killed Edward Chavin. Unfortunately, as I told you before, those prints aren't on file."

"I guess the one very good thing about it," I said, "is that if I find the guy with those fingerprints, I've solved two murders instead of one."

"Are you making any progress?" Dick asked.

"Not as much as I'd like," I said. "I'm still not certain what the motivation is."

"Well, happy hunting," said Dick and ended the call.

I hung up and turned to find Cst. Johnson walking up the aisle between the desks towards me. "I'm here to report on what I've found out about the Garber's Bakery van," he said.

"Did you find out much?" I asked hopefully.

"Do you want the good news first or the bad news?" Johnson asked.

"I much prefer good news only, but you'd better tell me the bad news first," I said. I was getting to be like Chief Bedgegood.

"Well, we found the owner of the van," he said.

"That's good news," I said.

"It would be, if it hadn't been stolen from him about six weeks ago," said the constable. "He's really glad to be getting it back undamaged, but he doesn't much like the paint job. He's a plumber not a baker."

I wasn't quite so happy with that news. "Did he file a report about his truck being stolen?" I asked.

"Yes, he did," said Johnson.

"Okay, now you promised me some good news," I said.

"Yes sir. We did an exhaustive search of the van in the police shop, including the wheel wells and under the hood. We also carefully examined the stolen goods. We got lucky; we found part of an envelope that had gotten wedged up under the passenger seat of the van. It appears that, when whoever unloaded the van grabbed the envelope, part of the envelope got caught on the bottom of the underside of the seat and tore off. There were no fingerprints on the paper, but I wrote down what was written on it."

Cst. Johnson handed me a sheet of paper. It had an Emery Street address on it that I recognized.

I smiled, and, now greatly relieved, Cst. Johnson smiled as well. This was an honest break.

Cst. Carmichael appeared beside us then and said, "What are you guys wearing goofy grins about?"

"Watch your manners, Carmichael," I said, "or I'll have you busted down to constable."

A look of perplexity passed over Cst. Carmichael's face, which made Johnson and I laugh. Then he realized the joke and laughed along with us.

"What have you got for me, Constable?" I said when we'd recovered ourselves.

"Getting that list of stolen antiques wasn't as much of a challenge as I thought it might be," said Cst. Carmichael. "When we visited Alice Mulder, she said she already had a list for me because she'd prepared a list for the insurance company. The only difficulty we had talking to Alice was getting a word in edgewise. We finally had to fake an emergency call to get away. But we did get the list."

We all chuckled at that. I remembered my Alice Mulder marathon interview very well.

Cst. Carmichael continued. "It was even easier to pick up lists from Barbara Watkins and Celeste Bedgegood. Mrs. Watkins is very organized and keeps an inventory of her possessions. And I think the chief must've phoned his aunt ahead of time because she had a list ready for me at the door. So, by the end of the day Monday, we had three lists."

"What about the lists from Irma Chavin, Martha Brightman, and Marian McKelvie?" I asked.

"I have good news there too. We visited the Chavin and McKelvie residences late Monday afternoon and asked if they could prepare a list for us. They said they'd be happy to. Both women phoned us yesterday saying we could pick up their list. So I have all the lists here," said Carmichael, handing me a folder.

"And Mrs. Brightman?" I asked.

"Oh, yeah. We asked her if she'd noticed anything missing and she told us she hadn't. So there's no list from her."

This was going much better than I expected. Since the Brightmans were the only couple who hadn't yet hosted a séance, and they also weren't missing anything, that provided corroboration for my theory that Dr. Plimpton was behind it. Perhaps he had a third associate, one other than the twins Simon and Simone, who worked behind the scenes while the séances were being conducted. An associate that liked to wear blonde wigs. She could be the one responsible for hiring local talent.

"I'm having a great morning," I said to the constables, "and I'm expecting to have a very good afternoon. I want you two to report back to me right after lunch, at one o'clock, because we're going to go visit a man I know who lives on Emery Street. I hope to have a warrant from Judge Henley by that time. We're going to enter the house and the garage to look for stolen property."

We took two police cruisers on our trip over to Emery Street. I rode with Cst. Carmichael, and Cst. Johnson rode alone. I planned to make an arrest, or at the very least, bring someone back for questioning.

On the way, Cst. Carmichael asked, "How's the baby boy?"

"Arthur Edward's doing well, and so is Georgie," I said. "They're supposed to come home Friday afternoon. Grandma Ethel plans to stay for a week to help out."

Cst. Carmichael and I continued our chat until we arrived at Kurtis Donnelly's home on Emery Street. He pulled the cruiser up in front of the house, and Cst. Johnson pulled up and parked behind us.

"It doesn't look like anybody's home, sir," said Carmichael. "Didn't you say they had kids?"

"Yeah, they have four. Two older children, who are no longer living at home, and two younger daughters. It's a Wednesday afternoon. The last day of school is this Friday, so they won't be here," I said.

Cst. Johnson got out of his vehicle and walked up to our cruiser, leaning over the passenger window.

"You go and knock on the front door, Carmichael," I said. "Johnson, you walk around the far side of the house. I'll go around this side, and I'll take a peek in the garage window."

Carmichael walked up to the front of the house. He knocked on the front door but received no answer. As Carmichael turned and looked toward me, the neighbour next door came out of her front door and said, "They're not home."

"Do you know where they went?" I asked, approaching the neighbour, a dowdy woman in her sixties.

"No. When I saw them packing up last Friday night, Sally told me it was supposed to be a lovely weekend, so they were all going camping. They haven't come home yet. When I saw you fellows pull up, I thought maybe there'd been an accident or something."

"That's not why we're here," I said. "We need to contact them as soon as possible. Do you know how I might be able to reach them? It's about a family emergency."

I was fudging the truth a little, but it wasn't exactly a lie because I knew Kurtis's aunt Celeste and her friends desperately wanted their antiques back. And with two murders in such close proximity to the thefts, I wasn't taking any chances.

"I'm sorry, I don't, they just said they were going camping," said the neighbour.

"I have a warrant to enter the premises," I said to the neighbour, taking it out of my pocket and holding it up. "We're going to go into the house to see if we can find any information about where they may have gone."

"It must be serious, then," said the neighbour. "I can help you get in. Sally left a key with me some time ago in case of an emergency. If you wait a minute, I'll go get it."

The woman disappeared inside her house and was back in a couple of minutes with the key. She began walking over to the Donnellys'.

"I'm sorry, but you can't go in the house," I said, stopping her. "This is police business. I'd like you to return to your home."

"Oh, all right," said the neighbour, handing me the key. "I hope they're okay."

As we searched the house, it quickly became apparent that the Donnellys weren't planning to return. The dresser drawers and closets were open, and clothes appeared to be missing. But they obviously didn't have room to take their loot with them. We found piles of antiques, including biscuit boxes, in the cellar, and more stolen goods in the garage.

By three o'clock, we were done with our search. I told Cst. Johnson to remain at the site and Cst. Carmichael and I went back to the police station. I had to talk to Chief Bedgegood.

I wasn't sure how this meeting was going to go. It'd been about three weeks since the chief had called me into his office to ask me to investigate the crime that may have been perpetrated against his aunt Celeste. When I'd reported back to him that a valuable antique and important papers had been stolen, he'd become apoplectic. Now I was about to tell him that the thief was his own cousin Kurtis Donnelly. It was with trepidation that I entered his office.

"Good afternoon, sir," I said.

"I guess you have a report for me," Chief Bedgegood said expectantly. He was sitting at his desk, doing paperwork.

"Yes," I replied, clearing my throat.

"Good," he said, signing a report. "I talked to Dick Robinson briefly this morning. He mentioned that you'd found the knife that had been used to murder Roger Watkins. That's good news. What else do you have to tell me?"

"There's nothing else new on the murder front at the moment, sir," I replied, "but I made some very good progress in finding the antiques that have been stolen during the séances."

"So you were able to track that bakery van down then?" he said, looking up.

"Yes sir, we found an address stuck up under the front passenger seat of the van. It took us to a house on Emery Street."

Chief Bedgegood furrowed his brow and set down his pen.

"That street name is familiar to me, Det. Franklin. Should I start to get angry? Do I need my blood pressure pills?"

"I would take a pill, sir, if I were you," I said.

"That damned Kurtis!" Chief Bedgegood yelled, pounding the desk.

The yelling wasn't new to me, but I was taken aback by his language. I had never heard the chief use profanity before.

"Are you certain?" he shouted, not quite as loudly.

"I'm sure, sir," I said.

"Have you arrested him?"

"No—"

"Why not?!" he shouted, interrupting me. His volume was set at the highest level.

I took a step back from his desk.

"There's nobody home, sir. They've all left. The house is empty."

The chief didn't shout this time. He pounded his desk once and leaned back in his chair. He rubbed his forehead and said, "Why would he do such a mindless thing?"

He was silent for a minute, ruminating.

"You might as well go now," he said finally.

"Sir, just one question," I said.

The chief nodded.

"A lot of the stolen goods are at the house, either in the cellar or the garage, and I have lists from each of the women who reported antiques stolen. Can I let each of them attend the scene and, with proper identification, collect their stolen articles? I'll have them sign a receipt that lists the property that they've retrieved."

"These are all prominent people," Chief Bedgegood replied. "I don't think they're going to steal from one another. I think I'll permit that, provided that only one of them attends at a time."

"With your permission then, sir, I'll have Csts. Carmichael and Johnson help me with that tomorrow."

The chief nodded. "Oh, by the way," he added, "will I see you at the Brightmans' séance tonight?"

"I briefly considered not going, sir, but I know your aunt Celeste is counting on me as an escort, and I know that Georgie is counting on me to collect all the gossip."

Chief Bedgegood chuckled, in somewhat better spirits.

"I'm sure you and I won't be the only reluctance gentlemen there this evening, Joel," he said. "My wife tells me that this séance is one social event that everyone wants to attend. Especially after the revelations of the last two. See you at seven o'clock."

The Brightmans lived on Queens Ave., close to downtown London, in a beautiful Queen Anne Victorian mansion with lavender shingles. It was much grander than Celeste's house, a full four storeys with turrets and second-floor balconies and ironwork railings. There wasn't a lot of parking for guests; fortunately, there was a prominent funeral home nearby that had a very large parking lot. The lot was almost across the street from the Brightmans' mansion, and easily accessed from Queens, so it provided very convenient parking for the séance.

The séance was being held in a small drawing room on the north side of the house. This room had large windows that would be opened this evening to accommodate a large crowd that would be seated outside on the lawn of the yard next to that side of the house. Dr. Plimpton had reluctantly agreed to use a microphone during his presentation of the séance, and the weatherman had cooperated by forecasting a beautiful June evening.

Celeste Bedgegood and I were driven to this evening's event by Paul, Celeste's regular driver, in his new Buick. Despite my negative experience on Monday, some intuition had compelled me to wear the Eye of Horus, and I currently had it on under my shirt.

We arrived at the funeral home parking lot and pulled in beside Marian and Butch McKelvie, who had also just arrived. We all said our hellos and then headed toward the mansion. Butch loved his SS Jaguar 100, and Paul was very impressed by the vehicle, so he and Butch were engaged in an animated conversation about its best features as the four of us walked to the edge of Queens Ave. Looking both ways, and seeing no traffic nearby, we stepped off the curb, with Butch leading the way, hobbling on his cane, still talking spiritedly with Paul about the Jaguar.

I was a step behind Paul and Butch, half listening to the conversation, with Celeste and Marion two or three steps behind me. I felt a sharp jolt from the amulet, yanking me out of my reverie, then heard the rev of an engine and a squeal of tires. I looked up just in time to see a red Ford roadster headed directly towards us at a high rate of speed. The car was about thirty feet from us; I could see that the driver was zeroed in on Butch.

I shouted, wrapping my arm around Butch's shoulders, and all but hurling him down on the boulevard.

Butch twisted in my arms as the car flew by, and let out a small cry, as if he'd been hit. The front tire of the roadster hit the curb and then bounced back onto the road, swerved a little, and kept going, leaving behind a stench of rubber. I heard screams of surprise from the crowd of witnesses and a stampede of footsteps heading in our direction.

I took a moment to catch my breath. I was alive. Aside from a sore elbow, I appeared to be okay. The turf of the boulevard had absorbed our impact. I turned to Butch and said, "Are you hurt?"

"I think I'm okay," he said, rolling over, "but that roadster took the shoe right off my left foot!"

I looked at Butch's socked foot and then out on the roadway at his shoe. I turned to look for Paul. He appeared to be okay, aside from some grass stains. He'd leaped for the boulevard and landed a second ahead of us.

I retrieved Butch's shoe and then helped him to his feet. Paul handed Butch his cane. Celeste and Marion, who had retreated to the other side of the street when I'd shouted, were just now beginning to hurry across. The amulet was once again cold and inert against my chest.

"Do you know anybody who would like you dead?" I asked Butch while we waited for them.

"Why? Do you think he was trying to hit me?" Butch said, alarmed.

"I certainly do," I said, nodding. "I saw the driver turn the wheel so you would be right in the middle of his grill on impact. But I'll never be able to identify him; he had on an aviator's hat and dark glasses."

By this time, we were surrounded by a group of people that included Chief Bedgegood. Celeste was talking to Paul, and Marion was fussing over Butch. I heard sirens in the distance. One of the neighbours must've seen the near accident and called the police.

"That was an impressive tackle," said the chief, clapping me on the shoulder. "You missed a career in football."

A police car pulled up, followed by an ambulance. A young constable, who seemed vaguely familiar, approached us and said, "I'm Cst. Brown. We received a report that a man had been run down, or someone had attempted to run him down."

Before he could say more, a man and a woman in uniform got out of the ambulance, came over, and joined the rest of us. The woman said, "Is anyone here in need of immediate care?"

"There's no need for an ambulance here," said Chief Bedgegood.

Cst. Brown, recognizing Chief Bedgegood, turned a lovely shade of pink, and stammered, "Does anyone have a description of the vehicle?"

"It was a 1937 or later red Ford roadster," I said. "Might have been a Model 78."

"You got a good look at it?" the constable asked, a little skeptical.

The crowd laughed, and the young constable became even more flustered.

"They're not laughing at you, Constable," said the chief in a kind tone. "The man you're talking to is Det. Joel Franklin, and he dragged Mr. McKelvie to safety just before they were struck by the car. He probably saw the car from about five feet away."

"Oh," said the constable, relaxing a little. He turned to me and said, "Sorry, sir, I didn't recognize you. Did you see the licence plate, and could you describe the driver?"

"There was no licence plate on the car," I answered, "and the driver was wearing a disguise: an aviator's hat and dark glasses."

"That sounds like attempted murder to me," said Chief Bedgegood. "Constable, get a message out as soon as you can for all the police in the city to be on the lookout for a late-model red Ford roadster."

"Yes sir," said Cst. Brown, relieved to be leaving the scene.

The immediate excitement over, we all headed towards the Brightman residence. I was walking beside Butch, who turned to me and said, "I owe my life to you, Detective. What you did was heroic. You risked your life to save me. I can never repay you for that. But if I can ever help you in any way whatsoever, please let me know."

I didn't say it to him then, but I thought perhaps tomorrow I would try to set up a time to talk to him about the Group of Six Investments Company.

Owing to all the excitement, Dr. Plimpton had no choice but to delay the beginning of the séance. Celeste Bedgegood, Marian McKelvie, and I were three of the seven participants who would be sitting at the heptagonal table this evening, and we had garnered a good deal of attention. By eight o'clock, people had calmed down, though, and Dr. Plimpton was ready to start the ceremony. His assistants, Simon and Simone, ushered us to the table and we seated ourselves in a prearranged order.

Dr. Plimpton leaned over the microphone somewhat timidly, as if he were afraid it might shock him, and said, "I have an announcement to make ... before I conduct the séance tonight."

The room quieted down, and soon the crowd outside quieted as well.

"I want to say a prayer of thanks to God for those who were spared serious injury, and possibly even death, by that runaway motor vehicle earlier tonight," Dr. Plimpton said, visibly rattled. "Clearly, someone up there is looking out for them. Please join me and bow your head in prayer."

Everyone bowed their head. His prayer was short and powerful. When he had completed the prayer, he said, "Perhaps this evening's events have increased the spiritual awareness in every one of us."

I was moved by the doctor's apparent sincerity. He seemed genuinely shaken by the attempt on Butch's life. I noted also, based on the prayer, that Dr. Plimpton's concept of Christianity embraced his ritualistic attempts to contact the dead. Perhaps Dr. Plimpton wasn't a charlatan after all; perhaps he believed in his séances too. I was beginning to feel I had misjudged him; maybe long years of practice had enabled him to con even himself. When does a con man stop being a con man and become nothing more than misguided?

Dr. Plimpton called for us to join our hands to complete the circle. He explained over the microphone to those unfamiliar with his work that this was necessary so we could communicate with the spiritual world. Simon and Simone lit our individual white candles with the purple candle. Once that was completed, Dr. Plimpton intoned in his best oratorical voice, "We are now ready to open a channel to the spiritual world." The Ouija board and planchette were ready nearby on a small table. Despite all the brouhaha earlier in the evening, Dr. Plimpton had captured everyone's attention and had effectively created an aura of expectation. The séance began.

As Dr. Plimpton moved from seeker to seeker, I could feel a response from the amulet. This time, it seemed to change in temperature.

Is the amulet changing, or is this an emotional or psychological response by me? I knew what Dr. Khryscoff would tell me.

Each of the participants asked questions, and each of them received answers of a sort, but there were no great revelations this evening during the séance. When the planchette was finally passed to me, I asked the question which was on everyone's mind, "Was the car driver deliberately attempting to murder someone?" My hands involuntarily moved the planchette to the word YES.

Aside from a murmur among the spectators about this sensational answer, this sixth and final séance conducted by Dr. Plimpton ended without a significant incident.

"That will be all for tonight," said Dr. Plimpton, apparently eager to shut things down. "The spiritual channel will now be closed."

The crowd grumbled, disappointed at the end of their entertainment, while his assistants snuffed the candles.

I talked to Dr. Plimpton briefly at the party after the séance.

"Where do you travel next?" I asked him.

"I'm returning to my estate at Grosse Pointe, Michigan," Dr. Plimpton replied. "I have a trip planned to Great Britain that involves eight séances in special locations, and I have to prepare for it. My first séance in England is in a castle just outside of London, on Friday, July 14th. I have a lot of work to do to get ready for that trip." He was clearly very excited.

"So, when are you leaving for Grosse Pointe?" I asked.

"This Friday afternoon at two o'clock; we leave from the train station."

He seemed to be relieved by the prospect. Relieved to be getting away from London, or to avoid being arrested? He may have been innocent of the attempt on Butch's life, but he was still my best suspect for the thefts.

"Had enough of London, have you, Doctor?" I said.

"Quite frankly, I'm glad to leave," he said. "There's too much bad energy in this town. I've never been so terrified as I was the evening of the séance at Barbara Watkins's. I probably wouldn't have conducted any more séances here in town if you hadn't talked me into it. I would like to have a longer talk with you sometime about your experiences ... at a later date. I sense you know something about the spirit world that I don't." He gave a weak but apparently genuine smile. "I confess, I'm also a little embarrassed about the rumours of organized thefts taking place during the conduct of my séances."

I was taken aback by his willingness to broach the subject. "Where did you hear that?" I said.

"Last evening. The Brightmans invited me for supper. They told me that all the people that had had séances conducted in their homes had been asked to provide a list of antiques or collectors' items that may have been stolen. They hired security for tonight's event, though you probably didn't notice them. They were dressed like guests.

"Let me assure you, Det. Franklin, that Simon, Simone, and I had absolutely nothing to do with any theft that may have occurred. We'll give you any help we can to dispel that notion. I can't have that kind of notoriety associated with me. It's even worse than the murder and supernatural phenomena. It would put an end to my business."

Dr. Plimpton turned to speak to someone else, and I stepped out onto the front porch to get a breath of fresh air. My conversation with Dr. Plimpton had left me feeling that he may not have had any involvement with the thefts after all. He was a pompous, snake-oil-peddling showboat, but he didn't appear to be hiding anything.

As I stood looking out at the grounds, a police cruiser pulled into the drive and young Cst. Brown got out of the vehicle. He looked at me a little nervously and then approached me.

"I thought I should let you know as soon as possible, sir, that we found a 1938 red Ford roadster with no licence plates. It was parked on Wellington Street about eight blocks from here. There was an aviator's hat and a pair of sunglasses in the front seat."

"Good work, Constable," I said. I had finally placed where I'd seen him before. "It's Freddy, right? We worked together on the manhunt for Dr. Khryscoff in Georgian Bay."

"That's right, Detective," said Cst. Brown, smiling.

It had been a little over two months since Cst. Brown and I had shared a boat ride to the island that Heinrich Smith was holding Dr. Khryscoff hostage on. Everything had happened so quickly that day, and I'd been so preoccupied with rescuing Alfred, that I hadn't really had a chance to speak to him.

"Well, keep up the good work," I said.

Cst. Brown nodded and got back in his vehicle. He looked much more relaxed than when he'd arrived.

Thursday, June 29th

I planned to spend most of the day at Kurtis Donnelly's house on Emery Street, helping the older women recover their stolen goods. This would probably be a two-day event. It would also give me an opportunity to informally interview the five victims.

Among the items we found were Etruscan vases, a 16th century Bohemian crystal decanter, a Ming dynasty tea set, a complete collection of Wedgewood chinaware, several complete sets of silverware, ornate Baroque candle holders, 17th century lockets with miniature portraits, gold and silver watches, ruby earrings, Renaissance hairbrushes and combs, diamond cufflinks, strings of pearls, a hand-carved ivory shaving set, jewelled hairpins, a gold-plated handheld mirror, 18th century clocks, two Swiss music boxes, an Amati violin, a pair of engraved dueling pistols, a Persian chess set, carved African figurines, Peruvian jade sculptures, over a dozen leatherbound rare first-edition books in various languages, three coin collections, half a dozen porcelain dolls, and countless other knickknacks and baubles, the value of which was often obscure to me. And, of course, a large collection of British biscuit boxes.

I wouldn't have known what half of these items were if I hadn't been able to refer to the lists provided by the women they'd belonged to, and I could only guess at what they were worth. Judging by the size of the homes they'd come from, I guessed a lot.

Since the thefts were occurring during the séances, they had to be portable, which meant there was no furniture nor any large paintings. Removing the found goods from Emery Street and returning them to the rightful owners, therefore, didn't require moving vans or trucks of any kind. I had arranged to have boxes of varying sizes and packing materials available at the site, however, as I knew these materials would be required when it came time for the women and their helpers to pick up their goods for return to their homes.

I'd scheduled times for the pickups in advance. To be on the safe side, I was allotting each of the women two hours, with a bit of a buffer in between. Celeste Bedgegood was first on the list and was scheduled to arrive at ten o'clock in the morning. Irma Chavin would arrive at one in the afternoon, and Marian McKelvie at four. Barbara Watkins was slotted for ten o'clock Friday morning, with Alice Mulder arriving at two Friday afternoon.

Celeste arrived promptly at ten o'clock in the morning in the Buick, accompanied by her informal chauffeur, Paul. When Celeste found me in the front room of Donnelly's home, she said, "You're becoming a famous detective, Mr. Franklin."

"Please tell Chief Bedgegood that," I said.

"Oh, Bubbles has heard me singing your praises," she said with a wink. "You have more talent than I thought you had when I first met you. I thought you were a bumbler then—you didn't even know which side of a person to sit on—but now I've seen you keep a cool head in the line of fire, not intimidated by wrathful spirits or speeding automobiles. Last night you showed yourself to be a real hero when you saved Butch's life."

"Please tell my wife that," I said.

Celeste let out a hearty chuckle.

"How is your wife, Georgie? And your little girl? Annie, as I recall. And that dear baby boy, Arthur Edward?"

"They're all good," I said. "Thank you for asking."

"Well, they'll keep you on your toes," she said. "Even heroes must bow to the whims of their families. Anyway, let's get on with it."

"Did you remember to bring your list?" I asked.

"I certainly did," she said, flourishing a little leather notebook. "Where do we start?"

"We'll start with the garage first," I said.

Celeste spent an hour picking through everything in the garage and identifying the items that belonged to her. She was able to identify who almost all of the other items belonged to as well. We crosschecked the items she identified as her own on our lists, then I escorted her down to the cellar. We had brought extra lighting down to make it easy to see what the thieves had hidden there and had made a couple of aisles by moving a few things around. Two steps from the bottom step, Celeste let out a holler.

"There it is," she cried, "my precious British biscuit box! That's the one I told you about, the one that had the documents in it. I'll be amazed if the contents are still in there. There were bearer bonds in there worth thousands of dollars."

Moving surprisingly quickly for a woman of her age, she hurried over and opened the box. She hollered again. "Jumping

Jiminy, it's all there! Those fools didn't even know what they'd taken."

She turned and gave me a big hug. "I'm so happy that Bubbles called you," she said. "Against all my expectations, you have solved the crime!"

"Thank you," I said, "but not really. I haven't caught the thief yet."

"Oh, that doesn't matter," Celeste said, waving her hand. "You got my British biscuit box back, that's what matters."

She took a moment and sorted through the rest of the papers in the box. "Here's something I don't need," she said, squinting. "With Compton dead these many years, it doesn't matter to me anymore. You can have it. Maybe there's something useful in it for you."

She handed me a document. It was titled:

Shareholders' Agreement, Group of Six Investments Company

I couldn't believe my eyes. In my hands was a copy of the document I'd been trying to obtain from the filing cabinet in Roger Watkins's cellar office. The one the company's lawyer had refused to hand over until he received permission from the board of directors. The last time I'd checked with the lawyer, he'd said the next board meeting wasn't scheduled until the fifth day of July, and since I had no way to validate that the document was essential to discovering the person who'd murdered Roger Watkins, I couldn't get a warrant.

I gave Celeste a hug. "Thank you," I said. "I've been trying to get a hold of this document for quite a while. I didn't know you had a copy."

"I'd forgotten all about it," said Celeste. "It's just the rules of some silly company my husband, Compton, set up in 1919. He found five other men and got them involved. He was a little older than the others, and he was the ringleader of sorts. He convinced them that if they all put some money together, they could form a company to lend money to anyone with collateral."

"Didn't you inherit Compton's shares in the company when he died?" I asked.

"I had the lawyer check it out," said Celeste, "but according to the shareholders' agreement, the shares revert to the company. Both the shareholder's initial investment, and any monies that accrued from it, become the property of the company. Heirs did not have any right to these monies. A silly rule for a silly company. But that was Compton."

"How much money did your husband put in at the formation of the Company?" I asked.

"Well, they were all wealthy men, you know," said Celeste. "Each of them put up $20,000. And that was in July 1919."

"Wow," I said.

"I told you they were wealthy," Celeste said with a grin. "They could afford to be silly with their money."

"So that's how you got to know Barbara Watkins and the others," I said.

"That's right," said Celeste. "We all thought it was a silly venture, but I'm glad they're my friends. They've been good to me since Compton died."

Celeste recovered most of the antiques stolen from her house, but her two most valuable vases were among the items not retrieved. She estimated their value to be in excess of $10,000. She was pleased with what she did recover, though. Her driver, Paul, and I were able to get most of her recovered goods into the Buick. He said he'd be back later for the rest.

It was almost noon. This was one day I wasn't going to make it home for lunch. I gave Grandma Ethel a call and then talked to Annie for a couple minutes on the phone. She told me Teddy wanted to go see Mommy and Rfur again.

Irma Chavin was due to arrive to look through the stolen goods at one o'clock. I wanted to have a brief talk with her about her husband, Edward. I also wanted to take a close look at the shareholders' agreement during the afternoon, so I decided I would use the kitchen at the Emery Street house as my temporary office. I would interview Irma Chavin in the kitchen, then have the constables help Mrs. Chavin go through the collection of stolen goods while I studied the shareholders' agreement at the kitchen table.

Irma arrived a little after one o'clock. She was accompanied by her chauffeur and by her maid Helena. She looked older than she had when I'd first met her, almost feeble. Helena helped her up the stairs of the porch to the front door.

"Good afternoon, Mrs. Chavin," I said. "I was wondering if I could have a few words with you in private before you look through the stolen goods."

"That would be okay," she said. "Helena has been with me a long time. She can start looking through those items while we talk. She'll most likely recognize anything of mine; she helped to make up the list the other day."

"That would be ideal," I said. "Thank you very much for that suggestion."

Mrs. Chavin had a short conversation with her maid, then we sat down at the kitchen table.

"I'm very sorry about your husband, Edward," I said. "I heard you had a very lovely funeral service for him this past Saturday. I'm sorry I couldn't attend."

Irma dabbed at her eyes but recovered her composure quickly. "Thank you, Detective. And that's quite alright. I understand you and your wife have a new baby."

"Yes, a little boy."

We talked for a minute or two about the baby, which seemed to cheer here a little, and then got on with the interview.

"There are a couple things I was wondering about," I said, opening my notebook. "I'm just trying to clean up a couple of details."

Mrs. Chavin nodded.

"The first question I have is about the séance that was held at Celeste Bedgegood's home," I began. "We've recovered the stolen goods, but we haven't caught up with the thieves yet, and even a little piece of information is sometimes helpful. Can you tell me what you remember about going into Celeste's office that evening?"

"I remember that quite well", said Irma. "I became ill during the séance, and I had to leave. I get migraines, you know. Celeste suggested I go to her office and rest. It's a small room, and it's quiet there. When I arrived, I found it stuffy, so I opened the window and sat down in an armchair. I had almost dozed off when a man came into the room. I pretended to be asleep because I didn't want to be disturbed. I wasn't feeling well, you remember. He went over and opened the closet door, then he saw me and turned and tiptoed back out of the room."

"Did you recognize the man?"

"No, but I think he was familiar with the room. He seemed at home there. He must've been a relative of Celeste or someone who works for her."

"My next question may seem strange to you, but it's important," I said. "Did you see a doll in the room?"

Irma looked at me as though she didn't understand the question. "You mean a child's play toy?" she said.

I nodded.

"No," said Irma, "I didn't see any toys in that room."

I paused, wondering whether or not to continue.

Irma looked at me directly and said, "You have some questions that you want to ask me about Edward, I imagine."

"Yes, I do. Are you okay to talk about him now?"

"I think so. I'm over the shock."

I hesitated, choosing my words carefully. It wasn't an easy question to ask. "Did Edward carry a flask with him often?"

Irma slumped a little. She sighed and said, "Yes, the last few years he had a problem with alcohol. He rarely went anywhere without a supply handy."

"Thank you for an honest answer to a difficult question," I said. "Do you know anything about the investment company that your husband and the other men set up? It would have been many years ago."

"Not much," said Irma. "It's almost like they'd sworn an oath not to talk to anyone else about it. I know that the last week or so before he was murdered Edward was really upset about something. I don't know whether it had to do with the investment club or not. Edward said to me early on the night of Barbara Watkins's séance that he needed to talk to me the next day about something, but we never had that conversation."

"Thank you," I said, "you've been helpful. I'll have one of my constables escort you to the garage."

I went to the door and summoned the constable, and Mrs. Chavin thanked me and left.

Mrs. Chavin's comments had increased my eagerness to take a look at the shareholders' agreement for the company, so I pulled out Compton Bedgegood's copy of the Shareholders' Agreement and placed it on the kitchen table. I picked up my 2B graphite pencil, ready to take notes.

The document confirmed some of the things I already had been told by Celeste.

> *1. On July 5th, 1919, the shareholders' agreement was signed by Compton Bedgegood, Edward Chavin, Ambrose McKelvie, Arthur Brightman, Roger Watkins, and Jordan Mulder.*
>
> *2. Each of the men contributed $20,000 to the purse of the company, creating a working capital of $120,000.*
>
> *3. The goal of the company was to lend money to anyone, provided they had collateral. The loans were not to exceed more than four years in length, annual inter-*

est rate a minimum of 9%. The interest rate would be higher if the risk was greater.

4. Upon the death of a shareholder, the $20,000 and any accrued profits would revert to the company.

5. Dividends of $4,000 would be paid to each surviving member of the board on July 5th of the years: 1929, 1931, 1933, 1935, and 1937. If all members survived July 5th, 1937, they would have received the $20,000 back they had invested originally.

6. The company would cease to exist on July 5th, 1939. The assets of the company on that date would be distributed evenly to the survivors.

I stopped reading at that point. Mathematics wasn't my strong point, but I quickly realized that a lot of money could be involved. I guessed that over twenty years the original $120,000 must have grown to at least $400,000, even subtracting the dividends that had been paid out. That much money was motivation for murder. That significantly narrowed my list of suspects.

It also told me that Arthur Brightman had lied about not knowing Edward Chavin. They'd both signed the agreement in 1919, which meant that Arthur had known Chavin for almost twenty years. Lying didn't necessarily indicate murder, of course, but it was suspicious.

Friday, June 30th

I was sitting at my desk in the detective section of the police station, but I wasn't being as productive as I ought to have been. I was thinking about Georgie and Arthur Edward. I was supposed to pick them up at one o'clock from Victoria Hospital. Grandma Ethel, our neighbour Kay Dunnigan, and Annie had been planning a welcome home party for the last two days. They'd been putting up decorations, and Annie had insisted that we have a birthday cake for Rfur.

Yesterday had been a good day for me thanks to the discovery of the shareholders' agreement of the Group of Six Investments Company, and it had been a good day for Celeste Bedgegood since she had recovered most of her stolen antiques. It was not a good day for Irma Chavin. The séance at her place had occurred prior to the séance at Celeste Bedgegood's; as a result, she only recovered one of her stolen items. Apparently, everything else had been sold or pawned. I suspected today's results would be similar. Barbara Watkins would probably recover her stolen property, but I suspected that Alice Mulder's antiques had been disposed of.

Just as I was getting ready to go over to Emery Street for the ten o'clock meeting with Barbara Watkins, the chief stopped by on the way to his office and said, "Joel, I want to speak you for a few minutes."

"Certainly, sir," I said. "I have a meeting scheduled with Mrs. Watkins this morning at Emery Street at ten o'clock, so she can recover some of her stolen property. If you'll give me a couple of minutes, I'll talk to Cst. Carmichael, and he can conduct the meeting. He can offer my apologies and tell her that I'll be there later."

"Good idea," said the chief. "I'll see you in my office in a couple of minutes."

"Have a chair, Joel," Chief Bedgegood said somewhat sternly when I entered the office.

Apprehensively, I seated myself.

"This started out as a simple case involving my aunt Celeste," he began. "It has now grown into a monster investigation involving both murder and attempted murder. Combine these crimes with sensational séances conducted by a man who is famous in certain influential circles, and the result is a story that has been commanding interest far beyond southwestern Ontario. So far, the *London Free Press* has been very cooperative, but now I have newspapers from Detroit and Toronto, and even the London *Times* from England, pestering me. You can understand my predicament; I have no idea what to tell them. You need to keep me up to date, Joel. I want a report *now*."

"I'll keep it brief for you, sir," I replied, trying not to stammer. "We don't have enough evidence yet to identify anyone as a suspect in the murders of Edward Chavin or Roger Watkins. I have my suspicions, and I'll be happy to share them with you."

"And the thefts?" said the chief.

"We still haven't apprehended Kurtis Donnelly, but we have put an end to the thefts that were occurring at the séances."

Chief Bedgegood's face became red when I mentioned his cousin Kurtis Donnelly, so I quickly moved on.

"With regard to the attempted murder of Butch McKelvie, we did discover the red Ford roadster and the disguise the driver wore. There is no new information on that as of yet."

"None of that's new, Detective," Chief Bedgegood practically shouted. "Have you found anything out *lately*?"

"Sir, I have brought an important document with me that came to light yesterday. Your aunt Celeste recovered the document when her British biscuit box was discovered among the stolen goods."

I handed the chief the document and my notes. He handed the document back to me without looking at it and said, "I'm sure your notes are easier to read."

As he read my notes, I could see him becoming quite concerned. When he finished, he said, "There's an awful lot of money involved here, Joel. I would guess it's half a million at least. That's a great motivation. The other big concern is the date."

It suddenly dawned on me that July 5th was next Wednesday. And every time somebody died, the shares got bigger.

"Yes sir," I said, pretending I hadn't been caught off guard. "We only have a few days to possibly prevent two more murders."

"We'll have to keep the remaining board members of that investment company under tight surveillance," said the chief. "The surveillance information I obviously can't release to the press at this time, but I'm sure I can give them a human-interest tidbit by telling them that some of the stolen property has already been returned." He said this last with the hint of a smile. It seemed that the meeting hadn't been a complete disappointment.

"By the way," said the chief, "the document in your possession describes what is known as a tontine. They are somewhat controversial."

"I can understand why," I said. "The last living person gets all the money."

At that moment, Insp. O'Neill knocked on the door. The chief waved him in, and the inspector said, "I have some bad news. Jordan Mulder was just found murdered in his cottage at Port Stanley."

The chief scowled at me and said, "Get those other two men under surveillance immediately!"

"I'll do that now," I said, shaken. "I'll go down to Port Stanley to visit the crime scene this afternoon. I might learn something that will be helpful."

Nothing, not even a murder, was going to keep me from picking up Georgie and Arthur Edward from Victoria Hospital at one o'clock.

I hurried from the station to my car and made it home to Princess Ave. just in time for lunch. The living room was decorated with streamers and balloons and a big hand-painted cloth sign that said YAY FOR MOMMY AND ARTHUR! Yay was Annie's favourite new word.

Kay Dunnigan, our neighbour, was there too. Grandma Ethel and I had talked last night and decided that Kay was going to stay with Annie while Ethel and I went to the hospital to pick up Georgie and Arthur.

Annie desperately wanted to go to the hospital with us, but we convinced her that she had to stay and help Auntie Kay get the house ready for Rfur. She agreed on the condition that Teddy could go in her place.

Georgie and Arthur Edward were ready to go when we got there. We said farewell to the nurses and the friends that Georgie and Arthur had made while they were there, then we headed out to the car.

It felt so wonderful to have Georgie and the baby in the car with us. Everything little Arthur Edward did seemed impossibly delightful to me. Georgie and Ethel had to keep saying, "Keep your eyes on the road, Joel. You can admire your son when you get home."

When we came in the front door at Princess Ave., Annie was jumping up and down like a cheerleader saying, "Rfur! Rfur! Yay!" Fortunately, Georgie had nursed Arthur Edward just before she left the hospital, so he slept through the cheerleading session.

Georgie put the baby in the cradle in our large kitchen. We had borrowed the cradle from our old high school friends Jay and Sylvia Jarvis, who lived in Chaseford. We had a cradle upstairs in our bedroom, too, that my mom and dad had brought to Princess Ave. It was the same cradle that I had used as a baby.

Once everything had settled down, I kissed Georgie and said, "I'm on my way to Port Stanley to look at a dead body. I'll be back for the party at five."

Georgie smiled sweetly and said, "You have all the fun. But I'm so tired I probably won't even know you're gone."

Since I was on official police business, I swapped my car for a police cruiser at the station. From there, it only took me forty minutes to arrive at Port Stanley on Highway 4. I had an address for the cottage, but I didn't know how to get there. As I had discovered early in my career, the best way to find out where someone lives in any small town or village is to ask at a local store.

I pulled up outside of VIC'S GROCERY and went in. Unsurprisingly, the grocer's name was Vic.

"You're lucky you stopped here and asked me," Vic said with a friendly smile. "It's kinda tricky to get there. Do you know where the beach is?"

"Yes, I've been there a few times," I said.

"Well, don't go that way, it's nowhere near the beach," he said. "S'matter a fact, it's on the other side of the harbour. Do you think you can get there?"

"Yes, I've been on the other side of the harbour before."

"Well, I'm glad of that," Vic said, "because it makes it much easier. You seem like a bright young man, so I think I can just draw a little map that should get you safely there."

He tore off a scrap of parcel paper and drew some sketchy lines on it with a stub of a pencil. "This here's the harbour, this here's the road," he said, pointing. "And this little X right here is the cottage."

"Much appreciated," I said, taking the map.

"Take care because there was some police cars over there this morning," Vic continued. "I don't know what's going on, which is a big surprise because I usually know within minutes, so it must be serious. If you have a moment, drop in on your way out of town and tell me what's going on." He gave me a wink.

I smiled and left. Clearly, he hadn't seen me pull up in the cruiser. Unfortunately for Vic, I wouldn't be returning to his store. He'd have to get his news the old-fashioned way: local gossip.

Vic had given me excellent directions, and within five minutes I was at a rather secluded cottage with a view of the beach. There were two cars parked in front of the cottage, one was a police car.

I got out of the cruiser and knocked on the door. A burly policeman answered and said, "Who are you, and what do you want?"

"Det. Franklin from the London Police Department," I said, showing him my credentials.

"Come in, we've been waiting for you," he said in a gruff but not unfriendly way.

He pointed to another man that was bending over a body; presumably, the body of Jordan Mulder. I couldn't tell for sure because the body was facedown. There was a pool of blood around its head. The man inspecting the body had wispy tufts of white hair and was wearing a tweed suit, bow tie, and thick glasses. He appeared to be about seventy years of age.

"This is the Elgin County coroner, Dr. Brock," said the burly policeman, introducing us. "Doc, this is the detective we've been waiting for."

Dr. Brock looked up with a smile and said, "Nice day for a murder, Detective. Well, unless you're this fellow." He patted the body affectionately on the shoulder.

"What have we got?" I said.

"The cause of death is obvious," said the coroner, pointing with his pen. "He was shot in the back of the head twice. It certainly looks like a professional hit."

I turned to the policemen and said, "Who reported the killing?"

"It was an anonymous tip. A note in an envelope came in through the mail slot of the Port Stanley police station this morning, a little after nine o'clock. The guy who runs the café next to the police station said he thought he saw a little girl put the note through the slot."

"If you ask me, Detective, I don't think she did it," said Dr. Brock, pointing at the body. "But you might get her as an accessory to the murder."

"Thank you, Doctor," I said, grimacing.

"We're trying to track down the girl," said the officer. "On the off chance we can get a description."

"And the neighbours?" I asked.

"No one heard anything. Not surprising, considering the distance between the houses," said the officer.

"Let me know what you find out," I said unhopefully.

I was glad I had come to Port Stanley because I got to talk to the coroner and the policeman face to face, but I didn't think I was going to learn any more today, so I thought I might as well head back to London for the birthday party. Thinking about Annie's insistence on having a birthday party for her brother, who was only eight days old, made me chuckle to myself.

I returned to the cruiser and backed away from the cottage. I drove down the laneway and pulled out onto the narrow roadway called Dover Street, the road that would take me back to the middle of Port Stanley. The Mulder cottage had been at the end of the second and final laneway on this street. As I passed the only other laneway that exited onto Dover Street, I saw a man I thought I recognized race up the laneway away from me.

"Son of a gun!"

I immediately turned and drove up the laneway with a steady rattle of gravel. I got to the end in time to see the man enter a small cottage. The car parked in front of the cottage looked a lot like the older Chevy that had been parked in the driveway on Emery Street the first day I visited Kurtis Donnelly's house. Two girls were playing in a pile of sand beside the cottage. They looked at me, startled. It's not often a police cruiser pulls up to your house.

I slowed down and stopped. Rolling down the window of the cruiser, I said in a friendly voice, "Would one of you girls please go and ask your dad to come out to talk to me?"

"I'll go," said the older girl, looking at me suspiciously. "Stella, you stay here and keep the cat away from our castle."

The older girl got up, went over to the cottage, and opened the screen door. Just after it snapped shut behind her, I heard a muffled conversation and what sounded like the girl crying.

Kurtis's wife, Sally, came out the door with her arm around the girl.

"Hello, Sally," I said. "I've been trying to track you and Kurtis down."

"I'd like to have a private conversation with you," Sally said, coming over to the cruiser. "Kitty, take Stella and go back inside and tell your dad that I'm going to have a chat with Mr.

Franklin in his car. Tell your dad to wait in the cottage until I come back to talk to him."

Kitty took Stella by the hand and they both went back inside the cottage. Sally came over and opened the cruiser door and climbed into the passenger seat.

"The girls don't know what's going on," she said quietly. "I'd like to keep it that way as long as I can. Stella's already very upset because of what happened earlier today."

This was almost too much information too quick for me, so I decided to sort through it. Keeping my voice low, I said, "I think what you're telling me is that they don't know you were stealing all the stuff that we found stored at your house."

Sally nodded and said, "That's right."

"I think you're also telling me that Stella is the one that found Jordan Mulder's body." That made sense to me because his cottage was next door to theirs.

Sally nodded again. They'd obviously hidden this information from the local police when they'd been questioned by them. Stella must have been the little girl seen dropping off the note at the police station.

"I think you're also telling me that you don't want me to arrest you and Kurtis here in front of your children," I continued, "but, rather, you'd prefer that the children be elsewhere when the arrest takes place."

Sally nodded again and said, "You're very perceptive, Det. Franklin. I told Kurtis we should've ended these thefts once you'd been to our house earlier in June."

When I took a closer look at Sally, I realized that she'd been crying. I wondered if it hadn't been Sally that I'd heard crying when Kitty went into the cottage a few minutes ago.

"How well did you know Jordan Mulder?" I asked her.

"He was my father," Sally replied.

I was dumbfounded. When I didn't say anything, Sally said, "You hadn't made the connection yet, had you? You would have, and probably quite shortly, once you checked and found out my maiden name. From there, you would have tracked us to this cottage. It was only a matter of time. I've been expecting you."

She stopped and sighed and, in a weary and sad voice, said, "And then this morning Stella discovered the body of her grandfather."

"Does your mother know yet?" I asked.

"Yes, she received a call from Chief Bedgegood himself late this morning. I know that because Kurtis and I drove to Vic's store in Port Stanley around lunchtime to use the telephone. I thought I would phone her in case she didn't know about Dad's death.

"Mom said she was coming to the lake this afternoon, and that she'd be here by three. Maybe she could take the kids into town to the restaurant before you take Kurtis and me into custody."

"Can I trust you if I let you go back into the house to wait for Alice to arrive?" I asked.

"Kurtis and I have talked about this. You can trust us. It's over; we have no other place to go." She got out of the car and shut the door. "We have to get this sorted out. We have to get the kids looked after."

It couldn't have been much more than fifteen minutes later when Alice Mulder arrived. She came by herself, driving a beautiful light-blue 1939 Dodge Luxury Liner. She parked beside me and got out. After a small shake of her head, she walked around to the driver side of my police cruiser and spoke to me through the open window.

"Good afternoon, Det. Franklin," she said. "Chief Bedgegood said you'd be in Port Stanley this afternoon, I just didn't expect to see you here at the cottage. But I'm quite certain I know why you're here."

I nodded. She looked away, visibly distraught, and I got out of the car to join her. We leaned against the side of the cruiser, taking in the view of Lake Erie. It was a gorgeous day, but I don't think either the sun or the heat did much to comfort her.

"My husband's murder has been a terrible shock to me," she said. "I'm afraid to go to our cottage because I'll expect to see him there, sitting at the kitchen table as usual, having an afternoon coffee. Jordan's murder, and this other terribly stupid business with Sally, is too much," she said, and she began to cry.

I tried to think of something to say, but before I could, the cottage door opened, and Sally and the two girls rushed over to Alice and surrounded her with hugs. They were all crying.

Finally, the initial burst exhausted, Sally wiped her eyes and said, "Grandma, would you like to take the kids into town to the restaurant for a treat? Mr. Franklin and Kurtis and I have some business to discuss."

The children were immediately excited, and the mood softened somewhat.

"That sounds like an excellent idea, Sally," said Alice, wiping her own tears and smiling for her grandchildren. "Come on, girls, climb in my car. We're going to the restaurant."

As soon as Alice and the kids pulled away, Sally said, "I'll go get Kurtis. We'll go with you now."

Kurtis came out of the cottage squinting against the sunlight and looking around. It was obvious to me he was reluctant to come, but Sally grabbed his arm, and he begrudgingly got into the back of the cruiser with her. I could smell the booze on him as soon as he closed the door.

"I guess there's no other choice," he said in a tone of utter dejection.

"We're being as cooperative as we can be," said Sally as we pulled away from the cottage.

"I'm aware of that, and I'm very appreciative of it. I'll do everything in my power to mitigate your sentences," I replied earnestly.

"I have another very important piece of information for you," Sally said. "Hopefully, it will help you solve my dad's murder, and ... maybe it will influence the judge to be lenient with Kurtis and me."

"What's the information?" I asked.

"It's what our daughter Stella saw when she went to Grandpa's cottage this morning. Just as she got to the lane to his cottage, a car came racing out of the lane and headed towards downtown Port Stanley. She said the guy in the car didn't see her because she cut through the trees, and he was going too fast."

"Did she get a look at the driver?"

"She said it was a big guy wearing a fedora. But that's all she could say. She did get a good look at the car, though. You may find this surprising, but Stella is very good at identifying cars for her age. When we're driving on the highway, she and her dad try to identify the cars as they go past. It's like a game with them, isn't it Kurtis?"

Kurtis grunted in acknowledgement.

"What did she tell you?" I said.

"She said he was driving a 1938 Ford four-door sedan with a Michigan licence plate. I wrote it down here," said Sally, digging inside her purse. She pulled out a piece of paper. "The licence was H 5603."

"Wow, that is great information," I said, taking the paper. Stella could give Julius Berton, another precocious child I'd met a couple of months previously, a run for his money. "Thank you very much. And thank Stella too. She'll make a great detective some day."

I turned down the road heading into town.

"I'm stopping at Vic's store for a minute," I said. "I need to use his telephone to get that information to London, so they can get an alert out to all police jurisdictions to be on the lookout for that vehicle."

After a short silence, I looked back at my passengers. Sally was crying quietly into Kurtis's shoulder. Kurtis looked, if anything, even more miserable.

"Sally, Kurtis, you're doing the right thing," I said.

Saturday, July 1st

Crime never takes a holiday, I repeated to myself several times as I drove to the police station that morning.

It was a beautiful, cloudless, warm July 1st. There was a big Dominion Day parade planned for downtown London at two in the afternoon, and a large fireworks display was going to be held at the Western Fairgrounds this evening starting at half past eight.

While the streets would be full of celebrants, my house would be full of friends and relatives. For them, the main event was a chance to see Arthur Edward, but they also hoped to take in the parade and the fireworks too.

When I left the house on Princess Ave., our neighbour Kay Dunnigan was already there, helping my mother-in-law, Ethel, get ready for company. Georgie was feeling great and helping in whatever way she could, but most of her time was taken up by Arthur Edward. And, of course, Annie needed some attention too. Annie helped Mommy by helping her look after the baby. Teddy did his part too as official observer.

My mom, Mae, and dad, Arthur, were due to arrive for lunch, and, on the telephone last night, my mother said my brother, Ralph, had just called to tell her that he had the weekend off from the RCAF base at Camp Borden, and that he hoped to make it to London for lunch as well.

I parked my car and entered the station. It was as quiet as a graveyard. When I got to the detective department, I found it empty.

ONE MAN LEFT

On a regular Saturday or Sunday, we ran with a small complement of office staff at the police station; on a holiday Saturday like today, there was only a skeleton crew. And yet a holiday like July 1st was a very busy day for any police force because of the parade, the fireworks, and the countless privately held parties, any one of which could get out of hand. Almost every constable would be on duty today, but not too many detectives were working. Depending on what kind of trouble unfolded during the day, of course, detectives would be working this evening. Unfortunately, I had some interviews to conduct this morning, so my presence at the station was required. But first I needed to see if there was any new paperwork on my desk. There was.

In the middle of my desk was a note folded in three with a paperweight sitting on it. The word URGENT was printed in large letters on the top of the note.

I unfolded the note and read:

Call Chuck Voisin, Chatham Police chief—thinks they have the shooter

Five minutes later, I was on the telephone talking to Chief Voisin.

"Good morning, Chief, it's Det. Joel Franklin from London. I have a note on my desk that says you may have the man I'm looking for in custody."

"I'm pretty certain it's the fellow you're looking for," said Chief Voisin. "Thanks to your alert with the description of the car, and thanks to one of my sharp-eyed constables, we have a man in custody. We knew he was armed and dangerous, but the car was spotted in front of one of our local restaurants, and that gave us an opportunity to prepare a welcoming committee for him. We nabbed the guy when he left the restaurant, still picking the food out of his teeth."

"That's great news," I said. "Do you have his name yet?"

"Larry O'Reilly is the name on his driver's licence. If he's a pro, that might not be his real name."

"Thank you, Chief, we'll have someone down to Chatham first thing Monday morning to pick up Mr. O'Reilly, his car, and his belongings. And hopefully his gun."

"Oh yes, you'll get the gun," said Chief Voisin. "When he stepped out of the restaurant, we had so many of our own guns trained on him that even a pro would know he had no choice but to hand his weapon over to us ... very, very carefully."

We exchanged a laugh at that, and the chief hung up. The silence of the detective department was broken by the sound of a band starting up somewhere outside.

What a great way to start the day! Next on my agenda was to interview the Donnellys.

I decided to interview Sally first. She was the one who wanted to turn herself and Kurtis in, so she would likely be the most cooperative. Then I could use the information I obtained from Sally to my advantage when I interviewed Kurtis.

As luck would have it, Cst. Carmichael walked by at that moment, so I invited him to sit in with me on the interview. He could record and be a witness while I did the questioning.

Once Sally had been escorted to the interview room, I introduced her to Cst. Carmichael and explained that he would be acting as a recording secretary. Carmichael would write down her answers to my questions, and at the end of the interview she would have an opportunity to look over what he had written and make any necessary changes. Once she had approved the report, she would sign it, and it could be used as evidence in a trial if necessary.

Sally looked very careworn and seemed to have aged overnight. But there was something else that had changed. She looked settled, like a person who is finally resting after a long journey.

I thought a little bit of good news might help Sally be even more forthcoming with us, and I was tempted to begin the interview by telling her that the man suspected of having killed her father was in custody; but I realized I couldn't do that. If that information got out, and we had the wrong man, it could alert the murderer, and he might flee.

So, instead, I said, "We're doing everything possible to track down your father's killer."

"My dad was a very good man," she replied sadly. "He loved his family, despite everything that happened to him. He didn't deserve to be murdered."

"Did your father know what you and Kurtis were doing?" I asked.

"Not unless my mom told him, and I don't think she did," said Sally. "He spent most of his time at the cottage in Port Stanley."

"When did your mom find out?"

"She didn't know anything until one of your constables came around to their house on Commissioners Road and asked for a list of stolen property. I wish I could have seen her face when he told her that you'd be contacting her to set up an appointment to view the stolen antiques at our Emery Street address. That would have made it all worthwhile."

I was taken aback by this remark and realized that Sally disliked her mother a great deal. "From what you've said, I take it you don't get along with your mother."

"I hate her," said Sally with a sneer. "From the time I was a little girl, I was never good enough. My big sister, Bernice, who was three years old when I was born, was the perfect child. My mother was constantly saying, 'Why can't you be like Bernice?' 'Bernice never acts like this.' 'Bernice always does what she's told.' On a few occasions, my mother told me she wished I had never been born. The hug she gave me at the cottage was for your benefit, not mine. I have to say, though, she does love her grandchildren."

In retrospect, Sally's feelings made sense. At every séance I had heard Alice Mulder ask how her daughter Bernice was, but until Sally told me, I didn't even know she had any other children.

"What was your motivation for getting involved in these thefts?" I asked. I was certain I knew the answer, but I wanted to hear Sally's answer.

"I guess it was a form of revenge against my mother," said Sally. "Kurtis and I stole items that her best friends considered extremely important. I knew that would upset them, and if it ever came to light that I was involved, then I thought they would partly blame her. I liked the thought of that."

"Tell me a bit about the thefts," I said. "How did you do it?"

"I talked Alice into inviting me along on at least one visit to each of the houses. I wanted to see them so I could learn the layout and know where their prize possessions were kept.

"You might think my mother wouldn't have invited me to go with her, but I told her my daughters would love to see some of these houses, so she was only too happy to have us come along. Like I said, she loves her grandkids.

"It was easy to find out where the important things were stored in the houses. All you have to do is tell people what a lovely house they have and get them talking about the furniture and pictures and stuff. Pretty soon, they're telling you all about their prize possessions. The older women were always happy to show off these items, especially to two little girls."

"Did your daughters know what you were doing?" I asked.

"Of course not," said Sally defensively. Then, softening a little, "Though I suppose they might have figured it out eventually."

"Who is Marguerite?" I asked.

"That's me," she said with a little laugh. Changing her voice, she said, "With this voice, and a wig, I became Marguerite."

Sarah had said Marguerite's voice was memorable, and she hadn't been wrong. There was something cutting about the way she said each word.

"Did you recruit Sarah Olson?" I asked.

"I certainly did," said Sally a little contemptuously. "It's easy to recruit someone as greedy as her."

"And the other houses—did you recruit people there as well?"

"Sometimes," said Sarah. "Sometimes Kurtis or I or both of us would pretend to be hired help and do it ourselves. If you're wearing a uniform, nobody ever asks any questions."

At that point, I terminated the interview.

Once Kurtis was seated in the interview room, I introduced him to Constable Carmichael and told him we'd just completed our interview with his wife, Sally.

"From talking to Sally, we know that the two of you were the masterminds behind the thefts from these properties," I said. "Sally and I also talked about her motive."

Kurtis sat slumped in the chair, staring down at the table. He'd sobered up, but looked like he had a nasty hangover.

I studied him for a moment, then asked, "What was *your* motive?"

"Do you remember when you came over to Emery Street and interviewed me and asked me why I changed my last name?" he said.

I nodded. "You told me your father was weak, and that you were angry with your uncle," I said.

"That's right," said Kurtis, looking up. "I didn't tell you all the details, and what you tell my aunt Celeste is up to you. I know she's convinced that Uncle Compton tried to help his brother. Well, Compton only tried to help himself. My dad was one of the first people that the Group of Six Investments Company offered financing to. My dad was a pigeon; Compton knew it, and the company took the farm. So, when Sally proposed this plan, I was all in favour."

"So your motive was revenge?" I said.

"Revenge, retribution," said Kurtis with a shrug. "The law was on Compton's side. What else I could I do? For me, it was justice."

"Do you know anything about the deaths of any of the members of the Company?" I asked.

"No, Sally and I had nothing to do with anyone being murdered," said Kurtis heatedly. "It was never like that. It wasn't what we wanted. But after what happened to my father, I wouldn't trust any of them. I think one of them is behind all the murders. I'd bet money on it."

"Thank you, Kurtis," I said. "I'm going to terminate the interview at this time."

Once we had the interview room to ourselves, I said to Carmichael, "Did you learn anything?"

"We found out the motivation behind the thefts—two people bent on revenge—and we got an unpleasant insight into those families. Those people may be wealthy, but that doesn't mean they're nice," said Carmichael.

"Before you celebrate Dominion Day, Constable, I want you to check on the surveillance in place for the McKelvies and the Brightmans. If my theory is correct, either Butch McKelvie or Arthur Brightman is in great danger."

Carmichael got up from his chair and I checked the time on my watch.

"Unless something happens, I'm going to call it a day," I said. "I've got time to get home to Princess Ave. for lunch with my relatives."

It was a wonderful lunch. Ethel had made a ham, and there was potato salad, bean salad, macaroni salad, and fresh tomatoes. There was leftover 'birthday' cake for dessert. We washed it all down with iced tea. There were eight of us crowded around the kitchen table, and there was a lot of talking and laughing. The baby Arthur Edward was in his buggy right next to the table between Georgie and I. Annie sat on a cushion on the chair on the other side of Georgie, and periodically she would peek around her mom and wave hi to Rfur.

My mom, dad, and brother had brought presents for both Arthur Edward and Annie. Annie was delighted. Sitting her new dolly on the cushion beside her next to Teddy, she asked, "Is it still Arthur Edward's birthday today?"

We all laughed.

We were all pleased to see my brother, Ralph.

"How are things at Camp Borden?" I asked, helping myself to another slice of ham.

"Training is going well," he said. "We'll be able to send lots of pilots when England needs them."

I glanced over at our mother. I could see she was upset by what Ralph had said, but she didn't say anything.

Our neighbour, Kay Dunnigan, said, "Do you think it'll come to that?"

"Unfortunately, yes," said Ralph. "Vincent Massey, our Canadian representative to the United Kingdom, gave a speech today from London. He said, 'To a casual observer, London might seem to be following its normal summer routine, but things are far from normal. Air-raid shelters large and small are evidence of widespread preparedness.'"

"That sounds awfully frightening," said Grandma Ethel. "Georgie's brother, Robert, is living and working in Norfolk County in England, not far from the coast, and when he writes us, he talks about how they're getting ready for war and, in that part of England, for the possibility of a German invasion."

The happy mood from a few minutes ago had disappeared. But Annie cheered us up by asking, "Can we have another birthday party tomorrow?"

We all laughed for a second time.

As soon as lunch was finished, Grandma Ethel said, "I know Annie wants to see the parade today. I'll stay home and look after Arthur Edward."

"Are you sure?" asked Georgie.

"I've seen more parades than I can remember," said Ethel. "And I could use the rest."

The rest of us headed out the door, loaded into two cars, and headed downtown to try and get as good a spot as we could for the Dominion Day parade. I couldn't remember the last time I'd seen Annie so excited.

Monday, July 3ʳᵈ

By eleven o'clock Monday morning, Larry O'Reilly, his car, his gun, and his other personal belongings had been brought to the London Jail by two constables, who had travelled down to Chatham early in the morning to pick him up.

I had been in touch with the police in Detroit earlier this morning because his driver's licence gave his home address as Apt. 3, 715 Poke Road, Detroit. They had no knowledge of anyone with the name Larry O'Reilly, and they informed me there was no such address in Detroit.

I wasn't surprised.

But I was surprised when I checked the registration for the licence plate for the car. The car was owned by Molly Ehrhardt, who did have a legitimate address in Detroit. Directory assistance gave me her phone number.

I called and a woman with a somewhat harsh voice answered. "Who are ya, and what do ya want?" she asked.

"I'm phoning about your car, ma'am," I said, doing my best to sound like an insurance adjuster and not a police officer. "Is it a 1938 Ford four-door sedan with the licence number H 5603?"

"That's my car," she said. "What did that idiot Jack do to it?"

"Sorry, ma'am, I'm just trying to make sure I got the right car. Is Jack's last name spelled the same way as yours?"

"Definitely not," she snapped indignantly. "His last name is Morgan." She practically shouted as she spelled it out for me, "M-O-R-G-A-N."

"Thank you, ma'am," I said, "we'll be in touch with you."

I hung up and phoned the Detroit Police Department again. This time, I got a much different response. The policeman on the other end of the phone said, "You caught Jack. Good for you. He's a bad guy; don't let him go. We have warrants out for his arrest for a number of things, up to and including murder."

Now I was certain I had the right guy.

At two o'clock Jack Morgan was brought to the interview room, shackled. I could tell Jack was a hard man just by looking at him. He was brawny and walked with a swagger, and he had a long scar running along the width of his forehead, just below the hairline. He didn't seem to be impressed by any of us, and that told me this wasn't his first time in an interrogation room. This was going to be a much different interview than the ones I'd conducted on Saturday. I had Cst. Carmichael with me again to record the answers.

I started by introducing myself and Carmichael, then I turned to my interviewee and said, "Are you Larry O'Reilly?"

He nodded at me and said, "Yup."

"That's a poor way to start an interview," I said curtly. "By telling a lie."

Jack hardly blinked. "You said the name, I didn't," he said.

"Do you agree with everything people say?" I said.

"Yup," said Jack with an insolent sneer.

"I'm going to give you a lie detector test then," I said, looking down at my hand, which I had cupped in front of me. "What's your name?"

He looked at me, bemused.

"I have your real name here in my hand," I said, wiggling the little piece of paper I had written the name on so he could see the back of it. "This could be your last chance before I send you back to Detroit. There are some people there who are very anxious to see you."

Now I had his attention.

"Jack Morgan," he mumbled.

"There now," I said. "That was easy, wasn't it?"

I let him stew for a minute, increasing the pressure.

"I'm very upset with you, Jack," I said finally. "You shot a man who was involved in an investigation I'm conducting."

"I didn't shoot nobody," he said.

"I have an eyewitness who says otherwise. And I have your gun, and I have your fingerprints all over the gun. To me that's pretty conclusive evidence. I've had people hung with a lot less evidence."

The word 'hung' had given him perhaps a tiny bit of worry.

"If you help me, I'll keep you in Canada, away from those nasty men in Detroit, and I will see you don't get the death penalty. Now, if you want to think about that for a few days while the fellows south of the border get their extradition papers ready, that's your choice; but if I were you, to be on the safe side, I'd cooperate with me *now*." I said the last word with emphasis.

After a lengthy pause, he said, "Okay, what do you want?"

"All I want to know is: who paid you to kill Jordan Mulder?"

"I'll tell you, but the guy has got money, and you have to promise to protect me," said Jack.

"You have my word," I said, "and I always keep my promises."

"Butch McKelvie," he muttered.

At first, the information puzzled me. It didn't make any sense. Jack had tried to run Butch McKelvie down on Queens Ave.

And *me*. Now I was mad.

Jack must've seen the anger in my face. "Hey, why are you getting so angry? I'm telling you the truth. That's who paid me to kill Mulder."

"You almost got *me* killed," I yelled, jumping up from the table. Both Carmichael and Morgan flinched.

"Oh," said Jack, realization dawning on him. "Honest, I wasn't going to hurt you. I'm a good driver. You and Butch were never in any danger."

Now it all made sense to me. *Don't believe everything you think,* I said to myself.

Until that moment, everything in my mind had been pointing toward Arthur Brightman. But he was *supposed* to look like the guilty one. Then, when he died, there would be no suspicion to fall on Butch.

But something still nagged at me. At the séance at the Brightman's, when I'd asked if the driver was trying to commit murder, the planchette had moved to the word YES. I wasn't sure what to make of that.

I looked at Carmichael and said, "You stay here with him, I'll be back in a minute."

I raced out the door to Insp. O'Neill's office, which was just across the hall. I burst through his door and said, "Quick, get somebody over to the Brightman residence."

O'Neill held up his hands and said, "Too late, Joel, Arthur Brightman's dead."

It was like a slap in the face. I didn't want to believe it.

"What happened?" I said when I'd finally recovered from my shock.

"His wife phoned about half an hour ago. When he didn't come in for lunch, she went outside and found him floating facedown in the pool. Dick Robinson, the coroner, and a couple of constables are over at the Brightman house right now."

It only took me fifteen minutes to get to the Brightman residence on Queens Ave. As I approached the front door, I was approached by Cst. Brown.

"Were you part of the surveillance team?" I asked testily.

"Yes sir," he said, abashed. "I was sitting on the front porch." He pointed to the chair near the front door. "Cst. James was in the cruiser across the street."

"What time did you come on duty this morning?"

"Cst. James and I took over at 6:00 AM," he replied.

"During the entire time you were here, did anybody come to the house?"

"A young guy came with a package for Mr. Brightman. I volunteered to take it in the house, but he wouldn't let me. The delivery boy said Mr. Brightman had to sign for the delivery, so I had Mr. Brightman come to the door, and he signed and took the package. The delivery boy was never out of my sight. He was the only person that came to the door this morning."

"Thanks, Cst. Brown. Is the coroner, Dick Robinson, here?"

"He's back at the pool, sir."

I went around to the rear yard and through the gate into the swimming pool area. Dick Robinson and a couple of other constables were there. Arthur Brightman was lying on his back on the deck next to the pool, his skin a sickly blue-grey colour. Robinson was still examining the body while the other two policemen were down on their hands and knees, very closely examining the decking around the pool, and the grass area adjacent to the decking, to see if they could find anything that may have been connected to Brightman's death.

"What do you know about Brightman's death?" I asked.

"Well, it certainly wasn't accidental," said Robinson. "Brightman has throttle marks on his neck. He didn't drown; he was strangled. And then probably thrown in the pool. Well, that's pretty obvious. He was fully clothed. Not many of us go swimming with our shoes and socks on," he added.

I could see the livid fingerprints on Brightman's neck.

"We also found this scrap of paper in his shirt pocket," Robinson continued. "I won't let you touch it since there is still a chance fingerprints might be found on it, but you can take a look at it."

Robinson held up a clipboard on which a damp scrap of paper had been spread out. I made out a blurred message that read,

We need to talk. Meet me by your pool in 10 minutes.

"Thanks, Dick."

I drove back to the police station. I wasn't happy; too many people had died in this case. And yet, as I examined the steps I'd taken, I couldn't see any other outcome. I simply hadn't been able to move as fast as the killer. Greed had driven him like a man possessed.

It was easy to get a warrant to arrest Butch McKelvie after the signed confession I got from Jack Morgan. Before I left the station to make the arrest, I stopped and talked to Chief Bedgegood. He needed to know what was going on. The story, which had been sensational to begin with, was going to become even more sensational with this last murder and the arrest of one of the wealthiest men in this part of Ontario.

I took Csts. Carmichael and Johnson with me to make the arrest. It was about two o'clock in the afternoon, another perfect summer day, when we pulled up in front of the McKelvie mansion, a ten-minute drive out of London. I had driven my family car, and the two constables had made the trip in a police car.

The butler answered the door and informed us that Mr. McKelvie was over at the new horse barn. I knew where the barn was. The police cruisers had been parked next to it the night of the séance when we had arrested Sarah Olson and Connor McDougall for the theft of the antiques.

We left the police vehicle in front of the main house and drove over to the horse barn in my car. As we pulled up, Butch McKelvie came out of the barn, waved hello at us, and came over to my car. He was wearing a riding outfit and leaning on his cane.

"What's happening?" he asked, apparently completely unaware of why we had come to his home. Or maybe he was just that good an actor.

The two constables got out of my car, and I rolled down my window and said, "We're here to arrest you."

Before he could turn around, Cst. Carmichael had handcuffed McKelvie's hands together.

I looked at Butch and said, "You're under arrest for your involvement in the murder of Jordan Mulder."

"You're making a big mistake, Det. Franklin," Butch sputtered. "I was nowhere near Port Stanley when Jordan Mulder was killed."

"I know," I said.

Butch looked at me, dumbfounded.

"Bring the cruiser around to the barn, Cst. Johnson," I said. "Load him in, and then take him to the police station."

I didn't plan on interviewing McKelvie until tomorrow.

Tuesday, July 4th

July 4th is an important holiday in the United States. There will be lots of excitement and a lot of celebrations. Though we'd had our own celebrations on July 1st, I was even more excited about July 4th here at the London police station. This is the day of an interview I have long been looking forward to. In my mind, Butch McKelvie was a truly evil man. A wealthy man who has everything he needs and yet wants more—and who will do anything to get it. I was certain his only motivation was raw, unadulterated greed.

I needed this morning to get ready for my interview, which had been set up for two o'clock. Though we had never recovered the container the acid was stored in, I was hoping to get some information about the fingerprints we'd found on the pocket whisky flask found on Edward Chavin and the knife recovered from the location of Roger Watkins's burial site. There was also the note that had been recovered yesterday from Arthur Brightman's pocket. However, Butch's fingerprints on that note could easily be argued away. I had Jack Morgan's confession, though, and Butch McKelvie wasn't aware of that.

Butch and his lawyer, John Dasher, were ushered into the interview room at two o'clock. I had asked Insp. O'Neill to sit in with me. Mr. McKelvie was a very influential man, and consequently I wanted to have an excellent witness. I also had Cst. Carmichael present to take notes. Unfortunately, I didn't have any fingerprint information yet.

Before I could say anything, Mr. Dasher, in an angry and confrontational tone, said, "This is a farce! As soon as we leave this interview room, my client is going to sue you personally, Det. Franklin, the London Police Force, and the city of London, for defamation of character. Mr. McKelvie is a very prominent citizen, and you have no reason whatsoever to charge him with the murder of Jordan Mulder."

"Thank you for your opinion, Mr. Dasher," I said calmly. I had dealt with enough lawyers to know bluster when I saw it.

I focused my attention on Butch McKelvie. "Mr. McKelvie, do you know a man named Jack Morgan?"

"No, I don't know anyone with that name," Butch said, hesitating for just a fraction of a second too long.

"Well, perhaps you know him better as Larry O'Reilly," I said.

"No, I've never heard that name either. Is he from around here?" said Butch.

"It doesn't matter," I said, "because Jack Morgan knows you."

"Everyone knows Mr. McKelvie," said Dasher impatiently. "Just because someone knows my client doesn't mean there's a connection between them."

"In this case, there is a connection," I said.

I couldn't resist smiling to myself. I was pleased that I'd had a brief second interview with Jack Morgan earlier that morning. At that interview, Jack told me that he had been really surprised that Mr. McKelvie had given him a cheque, upfront, for $5,000, before the murder of Jordan Mulder. He wasn't surprised to get the money upfront because that was part of the deal; what surprised him was that McKelvie had given him a cheque with his personal signature on it. Morgan still had the cheque. Or, I should say, we had the cheque. It was in his wallet in a storage locker in the London police station. I had taken a look at it before coming to the interview.

"I have proof with a capital P that your client Ambrose McKelvie knows Jack Morgan," I said. "In fact, I have proof that he paid $5,000 upfront to Jack Morgan for the murder of Jordan Mulder."

I think Butch must've remembered signing the cheque then because he suddenly wasn't as confidant as he had been, and, when I looked across at him, he lowered his eyes.

"If we go to trial, there is zero doubt in my mind that, despite your great skill as a lawyer, Mr. Dasher, your client is going to receive the death penalty, as well as a tremendous amount of bad publicity. I think you should take some time now to have a consultation with Mr. McKelvie. Ask him what written proof I might have in my possession that would connect him to Jack Morgan."

"You're bluffing," said the lawyer with false bravado.

"I'm not bluffing," I said, "but I am going to terminate this interview. I have all the information I need."

"You've wasted our time," said Dasher. "We've only been here five minutes."

"It certainly wasn't a waste of my time, Mr. Dasher. I'm going to have Mr. McKelvie escorted back to his cell now, but I want you to stay here for a minute. We need to have a very serious conversation."

When Dasher and I were alone, I said, "I have a deal to propose. Please hear me out, and don't make up your mind until you talk to your client. I will offer this deal *once*. It's good until four o'clock this afternoon. The deal is for your client Butch McKelvie to fully disclose his involvement in the murders of his fellow members of the Group of Six Investments Company. In return for his confession, I can guarantee he will not receive the death penalty.

"If Mr. McKelvie has a conscience, he should also consider the feelings of his wife. The wives of his fellow investment club members have been her friends for many years. Her relationship with them will be much better if he confesses fully now than if these grisly murders are exposed through a long, drawn-out, rancorous trial, where I'm certain he will be much vilified."

Dasher started to say something and then thought better of it.

"I'll remain in the building until four o'clock," I said. I was certain I'd have the fingerprint evidence by that time.

Lawyer John Dasher, accompanied by his client Butch McKelvie, arrived at the interview room a couple of minutes before four o'clock.

Insp. O'Neill, Cst. Carmichael, and I were waiting for them. I looked at Dasher and said, "Does your client want the deal?"

Dasher stared sullenly back at me and said, "Yes, McKelvie told me about the cheque. He knows he's caught, but he has some other good reasons for wanting to come clean. He wants the truth to be known. He's got something to tell you."

I nodded at Carmichael. He already had his pad and pencil ready.

"What do you have to say?" I asked Butch.

"I know this will surprise you, but I think you deserve to know the truth. After all, you did try to save my life, even if I wasn't really in danger."

I was surprised by his statement. It was almost a thank you.

"Yes, I did hire Jack Morgan to murder Jordan Mulder, and I did hire Morgan to fake an attempt to run me down on Queens Ave. If you hadn't shoved me out of the way, I would have dove out of the way one second later. But I had absolutely nothing to do with the deaths of Edward Chavin and Roger Watkins."

I must've looked dumbfounded because Butch said, "That's the main reason I'm talking. I knew if I didn't say anything, everybody's murder would be blamed on me. I know I'm a bad person, but Arthur Brightman is just as evil as I am. He murdered both Chavin and Watkins.

"One night, after one of our business meetings about six months ago, Arthur and I went out for a drink. We were astounded at how much money had accumulated in our investment company. At the business meeting earlier that night, which we held in the cellar office at Roger Watkins's mansion, we had celebrated because our books showed us a balance of well over one million. We were getting an amazing return on our original investment of $20,000, considering that the five of us had already received our $20,000 back in dividends over the past ten years.

"I don't know whether I mentioned it first or whether Arthur said it, but one of us said, 'If you split the money five ways, it's over $200,000 each, but if you split it two ways, it's over $500,000 in each of our pockets.'

"That's when Arthur and I started to plan the demise of our cohorts. We drew straws. Arthur got the short straw, so he had to go first. He selected Edward Chavin, and then I picked Jordan Mulder. We flipped a coin to decide who would murder Roger Watkins. I won the toss, which meant Arthur had to do the murder."

I felt ill as I listened to Butch McKelvie talk about this decision-making process as if it were a game. If Butch was sorry, it was only because he'd been caught. It did clear up one detail that had troubled me, though—Butch's cane. How a man who depended on a cane could murder Roger Watkins in a violent struggle, drag the body out of the cellar, and bury him, had given me some cause for concern, especially when I thought about the trial. It wasn't impossible, but it was enough to cast doubt on Butch as a suspect. Arthur Brightman had no such limitations.

"So what happened at Brightman's house Monday morning?" I asked.

"Brightman called me at my home on Sunday night and said we needed to have a meeting. We were being so closely watched that I didn't want to just walk up to the front door and say, 'Hi, I'd like to see Mr. Brightman.' I knew we likely couldn't meet without somebody else present. And Brightman had warned me during the call, 'Don't let the cops know you've come to my house.' When Brightman said that it made me really suspicious. I knew he was upset with me because I hadn't actually murdered Mulder but had hired somebody else to do it. He said that was cheating.

"I was afraid he might try and kill me, and that's what he tried to do. We were standing next to the pool, talking. The next thing I knew, Brightman was shoving me into the pool. Then he picked up what looked like a boat oar and swung it as hard as he could at my head. But I got lucky, I grabbed the oar and pulled him into the pool with me. He forgot that I'd been a wrestling champion at my school when I was younger. I got my hands around his throat, and since I'm heavier and stronger than he was, I was able to hold him under the water until he drowned."

"What happened to the oar?" I said.

"I put it back in the boat that was sitting at the back of the yard next to the cedar hedge. Then I went through the hedge, cut across the vacant lot, and got into my car. I'd left it parked on Dufferin Street. Then I drove home."

"When did you first meet Arthur Brightman?" I asked.

"Back when we set up the investment company. Compton Bedgegood introduced us."

"Is that when you met Edward Chavin, Roger Watkins, and Jordan Mulder?"

"Yes. Well, I knew Mulder and Chavin a little from the clubs, but I didn't really get to know them until after we set up the company."

"How well did you know Arthur Brightman?"

"Pretty well. As well as I know any of my business associates. I knew how he made his money and how much of it he had."

"Was this before your wives started holding the séances?"

"Oh yeah, long before. All this nonsense about séances started recently."

That confirmed—not that I needed it, since I had the signed shareholders' agreement—that Arthur Brightman had lied about not knowing Edward Chavin, and it lent a little bit of weight to Butch's confession.

"Have you got that all written down, Cst. Carmichael?" I asked.

"Yes sir," he said.

"Good, please hand it to Mr. McKelvie. I want him to read it, and if he thinks it's accurate, I want him to sign at the bottom of the last page and initial at the bottom of each of the other pages."

After ten minutes, and a couple of minor changes that we both initialed, I had a copy of the confession in my hands. I didn't like having to say it, but I did thank the lawyer, John Dasher, for his help.

"Before you leave, Mr. Dasher, and before Mr. McKelvie returns to his cell, there is one other piece of information I would like Mr. McKelvie to know."

I reached into my pocket and took out a folded-up wad of paper and held it out for Butch to read.

"Shareholders' Agreement, Group of Six Investments Company"

"I think you know what this is, Butch," I said.

"Yeah, I have a copy of it at home somewhere. It's not near as interesting as the books for the company that show the day-by-day growth of our funds," he said with a faint smile.

"I'm sure I'll get to take a look at the company's records sometime very soon," I said. "But, out of curiosity, how much money does the company have?"

"As of a week ago, we had a little over $1.4 million in the bank," Butch answered. "I asked the bank manager what kind of interest rate would generate that much money, and the manager told me that over twenty years it would only take an annual rate of about fourteen percent to compound to that much cash. I was surprised, but I'll be happy with $1.4 million even if I am locked up. And to think that this agreement comes to fruition tomorrow, on July 5th. I can smell the money coming towards me."

Butch was all but rubbing his hands together with glee.

"Well, I do have one more surprise for you, Butch," I said with growing satisfaction. "How closely did you read the shareholders' agreement?"

"I don't know whether I ever read it from one end to the other," he said. "There were far too many 'whereas' clauses in it. I trusted the lawyer and my partners."

It was hard for me not to say something when he used the word 'trust,' but I didn't; instead, I said, "Clause 17 is quite interesting, Mr. McKelvie. Take a look at it."

He read:

"Clause 17 - Criminal Activity

On the end date of this agreement only those members of the board who have not been involved in criminal activity are eligible to receive a share of the accumulated assets of the Company. The commission of a crime will disqualify any party from any proceeds from the accumulated funds."

There was a moment of silence. All the colour drained out of his face. Butch McKelvie had been totally blindsided.

"I'm surprised that a shrewd businessman like you didn't read the contract carefully, and I'm even more surprised that you trusted your partners and the lawyer," I said. "You have no one to blame but yourself."

I loved the sound of those words, especially when I had his signed confession in my pocket.

Wednesday, July 5th and Afterwards

Butch McKelvie had told the truth about one thing: he wasn't the only evil man. This morning I finally received information from our fingerprint man that the previously identified prints on the whisky flask from Edward Chavin's inside jacket pocket, and the prints on the knife that we strongly suspected had been used to murder Roger Watkins, were definitely not Butch McKelvie's fingerprints.

Earlier this morning, I had sent someone over to the Brightman's residence to retrieve anything that Arthur Brightman may have touched the morning of his murder or the evening before. His comb and his wallet seemed to be the most promising items for retrieving some prints. I wasn't likely to have information about matching the fingerprints until tomorrow at the earliest.

The scrap of material found clutched in Roger Watkins's right hand had been identified as a breast pocket from a shirt. The constable sent to retrieve fingerprints also searched for a shirt of matching material missing a pocket, but if such a shirt had ever been part of Arthur Brightman's wardrobe, he had already disposed of it.

Barbara Watkins called right after lunch to inform me that she'd had a conversation with the lawyer for the Group of Six Investments Company. He had pointed out to her the wording of the clause that dealt with the unlikely eventuality that there were no eligible recipients for the money at the end of the agreement.

Mrs. Watkins said excitedly, "Listen to this: Clause 21 says,

ONE MAN LEFT

"In the event there are no eligible recipients for the accumulated funds all assets shall be distributed equally among the heirs of the six original participants, unless one of the original participants has been excluded under clause 17, in which case the remaining eligible recipients will have their share increased by the appropriate amount."

Because of the complexity of the situation, and the fact that it was an ongoing investigation, none of the families had been fully informed of who had been charged with the murders.

I thanked Mrs. Watkins for her call. I was certain she'd be further surprised when she found out that, instead of receiving one sixth of the accumulated amount, she would receive one quarter because of the disqualification of Butch McKelvie and Arthur Brightman as legitimate recipients.

By the end of last week, we were able to match the fingerprints from Arthur Brightman's personal items to the fingerprints on the small whisky flask that contained the poison that killed Edward Chavin. The prints on the knife that was used to murder Roger Watkins also matched Arthur Brightman's fingerprints. Further investigation revealed that much of Brightman's wealth had come from his ownership of a pesticide factory, which had given him access to both cyanide and sulphuric acid.

What was even more surprising was the additional revelation we acquired indirectly from Jack Morgan.

Jack's cellmate revealed to us that, according to Jack, he had, in fact, been paid by Arthur Brightman to run down Butch McKelvie on Queens Ave. So the Ouija board had been telling the truth: Jack *had* intended to murder Butch. Jack had lied during his interview when he'd said we were never in any harm. He had been trying to double his profits. On questioning, Jack denied he'd said anything to his cellmate, and with Brightman dead, it would be almost impossible to prove his intent. But it wouldn't look good to the judge, and Jack's future was looking anything but rosy. How Brightman had found out about Jack, and about the deception, we would probably never know.

Celeste Bedgegood, Alice Mulder, Barbara Watkins, and Irma Chavin have all refused to press charges against Sally and Kurtis Donnelly. Celeste has been in to see her nephew Bubbles at least once every other day, demanding that he get the charges dropped. Chief Bedgegood has tried to explain to his aunt that Sarah Olson and Connor McDougall are also involved as thieves, and that they were all working together. It would be hard to get a conviction against them with the charges against their employers dropped. I'm glad I'm just an innocent bystander, and that he has a good supply of blood pressure medication.

I can barely hear him from my desk, but every now and then I hear his aunt Celeste very emphatically say, "*Horse feathers!*"

The end ... for now.

Joel

About the Author

Ron Finch was born in London, Ontario, in 1942. Upon graduation from the University of Western Ontario, he became a teacher of mathematics and physics and eventually became a secondary school principal. In August 2017, a month after his 75th birthday, he started writing his first book, *Lightning at 200 Durham Street*. Since that time, many other books have followed, and many more are to come. Ron has been a resident of Stratford, Ontario, for the past several years.

You can contact Ron at: ronsbooks@hotmail.com

Manufactured by Amazon.ca
Bolton, ON